Learning to Fly
a novel

To my mother and Beeg for being fascinated while you watched me write at the computer

Shehani Gomes

Learning to Fly

Perera Hussein Publishing House
COLOMBO

Published by the Perera Hussein Publishing House, 2008
ISBN: 978-955-8897-15-7

First Edition

Learning to Fly by Shehani Gomes
All rights reserved.
Learning to Fly is a work of fiction. The right of the author to be associated with this work has been asserted in accordance with the Copyright, Designs and Patent Act.

© Shehani Gomes

Typeset by Hanim AbdulCader
Printed by Thomson Press

To counter the environmental pollution caused by printing books, the Perera Hussein Publishing House grows trees in Puttalam – Sri Lanka's semi-arid zone.

One day there will be genuine smiles.
For the past.
For dreams to be.
For wonders to come.
One day there will be generosity
that will be enough love without clamour for dues.
One day wings will fly the way humans breathe.
Lost kites will find their way home.
Lost fathers their sons.
Bewildered lovers their deserving.
One day hearts will acquire love immune.
Cries only joy.

My praise shall be continually of you.
Psalm 71.

1

She ran inside screaming that rain had finally come and paper boats would be back to play. Kala examined her old books carefully looking for pages to rip out. Sumi came over giggling between large breaths, asking Kala to hurry before the rain stopped.

But the rain didn't stop. The rain boasted all it could. The drains worked quickly. The two friends danced away as each paper boat reached its destination. Kala's mother made pancakes for them with honeyed-coconut inside. K boats were lighter than S boats. And the K-boat maker bragged. The S-boat maker stuck her tongue out and held her breath as her boats hesitated. It was the weight of the paper, not the skill of the boat-maker that really mattered.

The last time she checked there was nobody claiming to be average. Everybody had something to talk about. There was no audience anymore. They were all Performers. Everybody had something different to boast about. So. She sought Averagehood. And reveled in it.

He cared about averagehood too. But more than that he was envious. Because he believed that he was below average. So he decided to believe in logic. Logic meant that he lived the way he knew without moping about the lack of averagehood. Logic meant acceptance. Logic meant there was no cause for morbidity over the below averageness of self.

"Dylan?"

"Yes. Why?"

"Sound respectful child. You shouldn't question back elders."

"Sorry."

"Where is your mother?"

"In the kitchen."

"Call her please."

Aunty from the Church had come to collect money for the annual talent show of children below twelve. What was the contribution going to be this time?

"Don't scream Dylan! People won't think any good of you!"

Last time it had been hundred. Two hundred this time. "Things are a bit difficult, but you know church things, can't refuse, no?"

"Dylan's still very small no?"

Mother laughed.

"Dylan can sing for the talent show," said Aunty from Church.

Mother laughed again and forgot about it.

Lunch: came in packets at Kala's place. (Did happiness come in packets?) Lunch was prepared the night before. For convenience. And stored in the fridge. The fridge that presented the possibility for middle class wives to play the dual role. The fridge that changed the art of cooking. Women who couldn't find jobs claimed that the fridge made the food dry and tasteless. Their husbands had an unusually vehement preference for unfridged food. But working mothers like Kala's defended the fridge and exalted its functionalities. So in the morning, food was served in packets and taken to school or to office.

Or lunch could be an entirely different story. Dylan got lunch from the hotel because he worked there. On normal days lunch was always normal. And nobody made a fuss about lunch or had pre-lunch premonitions of bad tummy upsets. Lunch was not an issue for those who let lunch be.

Dinner: Kala, the sister (who went to a special school) the mother and the father. With the food of course and the table cloth that was bought at the Church Cheap Fair the year Kala split her head after falling off her bicycle. Conversation at dinner was not strained or tense. Not that it was brimming with bubbles. But it was what it was. No conversation. Middle-class families couldn't afford conversation at dinner after a long day.

"Kala."
"*Kala?*"
"Yes."
"That's a weird name."
"No."
"Yes it is."
"What's *your* name?"
"Dylan."

"That's a dumb name."
"I thought you might know my name."
"Why would you think that?"
"Just thought so. How if we meet at McDonalds?"
She shrugged.
"Ten there on Sat?"
"No, ten thirty."
"Why?"
"I have classes till ten Dylan."
Shrugged back.

The sister: couldn't see. Before Kala knew what that meant she made fun of it. And then. She understood. The sister had a name. Nirmaleen. Tall for her age. Sixteen and two years younger than the older sister. She had beautiful eyelashes and those who didn't believe in creepy coincidences said that maybe the beautiful lashes stole the sight. The sister didn't believe that. But there were times. When the family went to church or to the Chinese restaurant at the end of the month. She was scared. Because she couldn't see who watched. And who cared.

The paper shredding ritual was almost therapeutic. So the mother came and participated.
"What happened wasn't fair. I'm sorry."
"Oh BLOODY hell!"
"Will you have dinner?"
Paper shredding became important suddenly. And little shreds were slashed until they grew tinier and tinier.

Eyes clashed. Then mother realized that all peace-making efforts were futile. So she left.

Nobody to cheer on or boo down mother's apology speech. And suddenly paper shredding became relaxed and leisurely (like the times Dylan took hours to make a kite when he was a child). So it was therapeutic. He forgot about it. Until he saw on TV the other day somebody slapping his girlfriend. And then he remembered. Slappers should be sent to hell.

Sat: McDonalds: 10.58

"I'm really reeeeee-lee sorry."
No fuss smile.
Well-I-thought-I'll-explain smile back.
Her hands are very thin "No fuss."
"Well I thought I'll explain."
"Draw what?"
"Draw *what* what?"
"The poster! Draw what Dylan?" *Ugly T-shirt.*
"I don't know. You're the artist. So draw some stuff - like you know - what they always sell at the Cheap Fair."
She had a high pitched voice that wavered slightly.
"Why pink?" *Do I sound nervous?*
"What's wrong with pink?"
"It's *pink*."
"That's all there was."
"Then we use red."
"Why?"
"Pink bristle board Dylan - I can only think of red that goes with it."
"Alright. Red."

"Girls know how to get about these days!"
"He has everything no? Car! Money! Race! Religion! And good job!"
"Not very pretty also."
"Our one can go for someone even better."
"Our one is prettier too."
"Our one can speak English too."
"Maybe a little later."
"No, she's old enough now."
"Our one is a bit backward though."

Kala pretended not to hear. How boring this marriage business. No essence for happiness. How bloody unromantic. She had no plans to rent space. There was nothing to let. No heart that loved romanticism. No eyes keen to flirt. How depressing if she married. She couldn't understand this compulsion to be glued to a man all her life. It strapped up independence as if it weren't important anymore. It made emotional parasites of women who started loving their husbands too much. It made a real life movie out of every woman who decided to give up individuality in a so-called marriage bond. Pathetic.

The sisters were friends. Because they were sisters. They shared clothes. But only some because they chose differently. Because they shopped separately. They shared a room. There were only three rooms in the house. And one was for the unnecessary overload of gifts that came from kind relatives. And then there were other friends. From the two different schools. And Kala was closer to friends in school. (Perhaps because they were friends who were not sisters.) Nirmaleen never confessed. But to her Kala was the best friend she had. Sometimes in a birthday card to Kala this was shyly (and almost casually) put into words since it could pass off for a 'Birthday Card Statement'. And Kala forgot 'Birthday Card Statements' that came from Nirmaleen.

Dylan had a secret passion. He never spoke about it. The secret childhood passion. He flipped carefully. He read in the quiet where nobody would come. Separating those that stuck together (since they were thin paper). He was embarrassed to admit it in public because it would have see med un-him. But there were the few who guessed or knew.

He read that night:

How lovely is your tabernacle, O lord of hosts!
My soul longs, yes, even faints for the courts of the Lord;
my heart and my flesh cry out for the living God.
Even the sparrow has found a home,
and the swallow a nest for herself, where she may lay her young
– even your altars, O lord of hosts, my King and my God.

Before the registration ceremony (where he wore a blue satin shirt) they had Bible sessions together. And she told him once that the Psalms were moo-si-kle and lovelier than anything else in the Bible. He had watched her eyes sparkle and whenever he noticed a similar sparkle he warmed to it, even many years later. The sessions stopped after a while since mother became caught up with the new adjustments - the husband and the lifestyle. But the Psalms remained musical because Dylan read them to remember God. And mother. And everyone else that mattered.

✱

"You like blue a lot don't you?" Dylan asked.

Dylan sounded too confident Kala thought. She didn't like pervasively confident morons.

"Why do you say that?" Kala asked back. Looking up and not grateful for the interruption.

"You pick it up and put it down again. And the times you pick it up, it's obvious that blue won't fit in."

"Hmmm." Shut up look.

"So why blue?"

"Because blue hides moods." Thin smile - shut up smile.

"What do you think of white?"

"That it's white." Vague look.

"That's what I think too. It's too white. There's no need to look hard."

"Hmmm true." *I need to bloody finish this fast before this creep makes a psychological study out of me.*

"Could you pass the black?"

"And black?" *She has blackheads on her nose.*

"What's with you and colours?" Light cackle - shut up cackle which Dylan didn't think was light at all. He thought of it more as a harsh noise.

"Nothing. Forget it."

Shit! Is he hurt now? Men are so bloody sensitive!

Kala cleared her throat, the way politicians did at mass rallies. "Actually I think black has moods. You know boring black. Ugly black. Sexy black. Sad black. Grand black. Black fits in." *Look up! Do something! I'm sorry!*

He looked up finally.

"I like colours. That's all. I think of them as little wizards who charm the world."

Kala looked puzzled.

"You asked what's with me and colours?"

"Oh. Yeah." She nodded hard. The way supporters did at mass political rallies.

"I just like them." He shrugged. Looked away. He offered to take the half done posters home.

She said "OK thanks."

"Sat McDonald's 10:30?"

"OK."

Kala and her girlfriends went to see a movie after tuition. The theatre was dark but the popcorn containers were white and lit up places here and there where popcorn lovers sat. The movie had been in the pipeline for a week. Meticulously planned. Planning which involved getting money for movie tickets and more importantly knowing what to wear. Clothes were the mover and shaker of the All Critical Thing which some called the mood. A huge board hung in red letters:

NOW SHOWING

MAD HUSBAND'S PRETTY GIRLFRIEND

Kala fell in love with the dialogue and the simplicity. They sat snuggled in comfortably. Sumi kept laughing very loud. The mad husband stuck with a sane wife kept shouting at her constantly. Then he found a pretty girlfriend. He tried to break away from the depressing nuptial reality. Then he was sad and mad. He made Kala sad. How terribly depressed he was. Depression ruined him to bits. Then he divorced the sane wife and broke up with the

pretty girlfriend when he realized that he cared for neither. And then he was in a car listening to American Hip-hop with a look of contentment. Curtain. People stretch. Laugh. Stretch. Queue.
Shit! SHIT! Don't see me! And I won't see you!
Let's try and ignore. No mood for PR.
"Going home?"
"Yes."
"At this time? In the bus?"
"Yes, why?"
"It's too late for a girl to travel."
"Why? Do men rape?"
"Yes they do."
"Where do you work?"
"Why? Why do you ask?"
"Just crossed my mind. But you don't have to tell me. I only asked because there's nothing else to ask."
"You travel late Kala?"
"Yes. Unraped as yet."
He smiled.
She didn't know what to do, smile back? Unnecessary. Very unnecessary. She hardly knew him. He was a chauvinist too.
"Tuition?"
She shook her head.
"Then?"
"Movie."
"What movie?"
"Mad Husband's Pretty Girlfriend."
"Good?"
She shrugged.
"That's it?"

"You should watch it sometime."

"Maybe I will. Can I ask something personal?"

"What?" *What the hell?*

"What's your favourite movie?"

"Oh. Beauty Born Bad."

"Good?"

"Hmmm." She looked away, wishing he hadn't made it seem so personal. It was only the favourite movie after all. Nothing in it.

"What's your favourite colour?

"Why?" *What the bloody hell?*

"Blue?"

"No."

He shrugged.

"Why blue?" she asked. "I don't like blue."

He shrugged again.

"Why did you like the movie?"

"Why do you want to know?" She sounded indignant. He backed off.

"Well. It's a really quiet movie," she began, as if at a peace accord. "And I like the characters. I thought there was a lot of underlying passion. And the theme - happiness being an abstract concept." She finished wanting to breathe.

He looked at her, but didn't say anything.

She started again "I liked the pretty girlfriend. She was tragic. Her lover wasn't romantic either. I liked the reminiscence."

"Remni-what?"

"Reminiscence. Like going back to what has happened."

"You use big words." Big cheeky grin as if he caught her kissing when she wasn't supposed to.

"Sorry. Didn't think it was one."

"No? Then how come I don't know it?"

She tried hard not to laugh.
"What's resonating Kala?"
Nonplussed. "I don't know... something like radiant?"
"I don't know."
"Then why did you ask me?"
"Just checking how much you know."
"It's a pretty word."
"What do you call camera lenses that can see far?"
"Binoculars?"
"Clever. What's an ugly word?"
"There are no ugly words. Pretty words and Just words."
"Tell me a Just word."
She tried to think of a Just word, but only Pretty words crossed the mind. "I can't think of any Just words right now." She looked apologetic.
"Oh! OK."
The bus conductor asked them to get down. Dylan followed Kala out of the bus.
"Yes is a Just word."
"It's too late for a girl to walk home."
"I like to walk home alone."
"Can I walk home with you?"
"It's too much trouble." She looked uncomfortable again.
"It's nothing. And I'm trying to be a good boy too." He grinned. She could vaguely make it out in the dark.
"Why? Have you been a bad boy?"
He laughed. "Have you always been a good girl?" He asked as if it were a very personal question.
She nodded as if there could be no doubt.
"I've always been a good boy too."

Dylan came home that night and read about reminiscence. **Reminiscence:** Story from the past that may be either enjoyable or otherwise. According to Kala - Reminiscence was a Pretty word. How did words become pretty or ugly, he wondered. He wore shorts that had lost their original blue and settled for a faded shade of it due to the use of bleach-containing washing powder despite a little care label that hung by the side that advised "Do Not Bleach". And a T-shirt with Elephants and the words Sri Lanka on top. It wasn't a patriotic T-shirt. Just one of those that became common without a patriotic surge. But he had Sri Lanka Cricket T-shirts that were patriotic. Cricket was the ultimate mark of patriotism. People stayed off work and they droned and groaned before large TV screens waiting for 'our boys' to show them up. Whoever they were. T-shirts with Elephants were a mark of the island's faint hopes of becoming a healthy tourism hot spot.

Funny woman he thought. Watching funny movies and trying to sound as if she knew everything. Sad little ugly girl. Spoke very loud too. Very sad little ugly girl. Rather pretty too though. Wasn't she? Was she? He wasn't sure. The only word that could even vaguely describe her was not-pretty.

Estrangement took place in middle-class families. It was known as a passing phase where the family ceased to be the nearest parameter. But estrangement was an ever so imperceptible threat that nobody talked about it. Besides Sri Lanka was a developing country that dealt with peace-talks, war and living standards. Sociological problems were only known in super-wealthy countries where people needed to be told what their teenage kids might be going through on news channels as a feature. The estranged were strange cases of Determined Self-Induced Reclusion and Almost-Self-Pity. The estrangers had no idea really. Except maybe sometimes when the occasional chat had lost its mirth. Then the brows would gather up to worry. And then the water and telephone bills would strike the mind. But occasional chats were occasional. There was nothing to worry consequently. Kids needed the telephone and the water. But those who knew estrangement knew that it was sad. Sad as poverty and malnutrition.

Estranged Case 1: Sumanthi

It happened without much ado (like it always did). That was how estrangement worked. There was no formal announcement, or there would have been polite/not-so-polite refusals. So estrangement came unannounced. In any case dramatic arrivals were rather old fashioned. Sumanthi was sixteen when she started seeing Pradeep. He was popular. Played cricket for school. Junior prefect. She did all the things that girls became popular for - school choir, English speech and basketball. Plus she was a smart kid. But he liked her face of course. Face carried a lot and it became an easy assessment tool of prettiness and hotness. Sumanthi was Pretty Hot that way. She had other connections as well. She was Kala's best friend. They studied together at the same school and estrangement began the time Sumanthi started going out with Pradeep. When they broke up - over nothing so much as cheating, but the maturing realization that it was a social need rather than an emotional need, this whole going out business - Sumanthi didn't know that her mother had a persistent cough in the nights. But the saddest thing was that Sumanthi didn't know that her mother didn't like flowery blouses anymore. And when she bought mother a flowery blouse for her birthday (one month after breaking up with her first boyfriend) it hardly occurred to mother that it may be estrangement.

Estranged Case 2: Kala

Perhaps in the post-puberty-era that made a young girl feel awkward. Concern became practiced. The same tone. And even the words. Worry too was practiced. Conversations grew quiet. Estrangement was sad. Because emotional needs of a young girl struggling with growing breasts and crude men were not understood. (How could parents remember what it was like to be an adolescent? So emotional needs were not perceived.) By eighteen, estrangement had taken its toll. Parents thought Kala was a quiet young girl - they didn't know how Kala screamed among the unestranged in school corridors, classrooms and playgrounds - and Kala played along. The most comfortable arrangement was to be called a quiet shy girl who listened rather than talked.

The Case for non-Estrangement: Dylan

Dylan had no idea what estrangement meant. Estrangement was a luxury enjoyed by those who had close ties and then decided to break away. In that he was a poor boy. He always had been. He kept records of all those who loved him and how much. He was sharp-eyed that way, because he figured Family and Related Associates were a rare species that was complicated to replace. And if he had known what estrangement meant he would have looked at the whole issue with contempt.

2

THE ELOCUTION CLASS BOY WAS ALL THERE WAS AT FOURTEEN. The elocution class boy was polite. Spoke well too. Kala wasn't pretty at fourteen, rather ugly. Kala hated having lunch after school next to him. She didn't risk smiling while eating rice. If he saw food particles stuck between teeth, that wouldn't have reflected well on an already ugly face. She only smiled back with pursed lips if he spoke while she had lunch or nodded without opening the mouth. Parents knew the importance of elocution for their children in a country where English was a class weapon. And a few children like Kala understood the importance of attending such classes and meeting its associates. At class Kala worked hard and cherished the few words she exchanged with the elocution class boy. She even had a word count. Most conversations contained thirteen words.

How are you doing today?
I'm good, how are you?
I'm good too.

There was the occasional extra question that would take the

word count to twenty two. There was such a difference between thirteen and twenty two. Nine words could make up a whole sentence, or even two questions.
Are you taking up drama as well?
Not really.

Such days were known as Better Elocution Class Days. They created optimism for weeks about everything else.

Nirmaleen first heard about stars from Kala. Stars smote Kala at thirteen when she studied about constellations for science. The introductions took place. And Nirmaleen and the stars became good friends. They spoke on nights reported to be not cloudy. Kala knew about the secret conversations. But pretended otherwise. Nirmaleen would casually surmise, "Today must be a cloudy night with these winds no?" Kala would imitate the casualness with a "Not really, rather bright you know." Nirmaleen had many friends who were permanent residents on stars. At sixteen it seemed perfectly normal to talk to star people. A typical chat with stars would range between invitations to dinner, to upcoming weddings to school assignments to sudden spasms of anger. Star people were wonderful that way. They heard Nirmaleen when she needed to talk. So on a Monday night when the sky was 'rather-bright-you-know,' Nirmaleen asked the star people over for dinner.
"But you *must* come for dinner!"
"What will your folks say?" Nirmaleen asked in a low baritone playing spokesperson for star people.
"They will like you! Who wouldn't?" she asked back in whisper.

And then she stopped. Embarrassed. She always stopped when

she sensed someone around. Her mother had told her that her other faculties were stronger since she couldn't see. Dylan peered through the low gate to the garden where Kala and Nirmaleen stood gazing at the sky. "Why outside? The breeze?" he asked Kala. "No." Kala looked up. "The stars," and then at her sister. "She likes them," in conspiring tones. Dylan wondered why women hid legs during daylight and wore shorts at night. It made no sense. He peered to imagine what Kala's legs looked like. *Can't see a bloody thing!* "After work. Thought I'll take a walk." "You walk at this time of the night?" Kala looked childlike. Kala looked disgusted. It was such a mix. "It's not safe!" He looked confused, amused. It was such a mix. "Why isn't it safe?"

"There are rogues." She widened her eyes as she made a point. The way professors did to confused university students. He peered down again trying to assess whether her legs were thin. Nirmaleen was wearing a long nightdress that made her look thin. They both stood in the garden while Dylan spoke over the gate with his hands inside his shorts' pockets. Kala was curious to know whether he was a hairy man. So she scrutinized his naked legs. She stared hard and made mental notes and came to the following conclusions:

a) Dylan had legs that grew hair that was approximately one and half inches long.

b) His legs were so to speak, shrouded in hair, causing Kala to remember Fred Flintstone.

c) Dylan had thin legs, which (Kala concluded rather simplistically) may be the result of excessive walks, like the one he was having at that point.

"Rogues can't catch Dylan the Superman." He showed off a cocky look.

"So you're Dylan?" Nirmaleen chipped in finally.
"Yes. So you know my name?" He showed off another big, Superman cocky look that made Kala feel miserable. This was destined to be a sad night when Dylan would find out that she had spoken about him with Nirmaleen.
"No, she doesn't."
"Kala talks about you."
Kala looked at her feet, they looked ugly. Very ugly. Nothing to stare at other than in moments of despair.
"Dylan, my sister Nirmaleen."
"This is Dylan."
"I know."
"Pleasure meeting you Nirmaleen."
Nirmaleen shook the hand shyly.
"I - uh - mentioned your name when I said that I might be late on Saturday after class, for posters you know."
"OK. I'll catch you on Sat then." He played out a fresher and stronger Superman-cocky smile that made Kala want to scream that he had the ugliest legs she had ever seen on a man.

Saturdays were looked forward to. Because Saturdays were fun. Because Kala pretended to be giddy on Saturdays. Kala spent hours trying to decide what Careless Outfit to wear. She always looked for a faded top that would create *Oh-you-so-don't-matter-Dylan* impression. Dylan stayed unshaven to look unshaven. The nicest jeans worn without looking dressy. He wore an old T-shirt that always complemented his stubble. Intent to look sexy without effort.
"Do women get nervous around men?"

"What?"

"Do they?"

"How would I know? And frankly I couldn't care less!"

"Why do you sound nervous at times?" He sounded nervous.

"Maybe because I feel uncomfortable."

"But why would you be uncomfortable? I'm a nice guy."

"I'm sorry."

"That's sweet."

"Will you be friends with me?"

"But I already am."

"Great! Thanks."

"Do you like to draw?"

She didn't say anything. Wasn't it obvious?

"I love watching you draw."

She was embarrassed. "Drawing calms me down. Takes me to another planet. You know how it is?"

"Are you in constant restlessness otherwise?"

"No. Just that it opens up a happier space within. Drawing I mean."

"Ah! Very spiritual."

"Is there something wrong with spirituality?"

"No."

"Why do women get nervous around men Kala? Are they born nervous?"

"Have you had a bad experience with a nervous woman?" She let out a cackle.

"Yes."

"You should ask her then."

"Just wanted some insight. You know?"

"Get to know yourself. Then it won't seem very important to

know what makes women nervous."
"You watch talk shows?" He winked.
"I'm too good for them!" She winked back.

"We have to go," Aunty Mangala rushed in. Aunty Mangala sweaty and tired with dark circles under her eyes. Dark circles under sad eyes that had been weakened by the shock of tears. This moment of loss. Shocked eyes that faked calm of calms.
"Where do we have to go?"
"We have to go home."
"I have a lot of work in school." Dylan spoke with importance.
"We have to go Dylan," she said softly.
"Can I come after school?"
"You may go Dylan. It's OK," the class teacher said for the first time since Aunty Mangala walked in.
"I don't want to go."
"I'll buy a play gun on the way."
"Dylan today is a holiday for you since you have done well at math," the teacher chipped in with sorry eyes.
"Really?"
"Yes."
"And others still in class?"
"Yes."
They helped Dylan to pack. He first put his English book inside. Then the Sinhala book. Then 'My Alphabet.' And the math book came out of the desk lastly like a king. The king who declared a holiday.

Before the thing happened everything had been normal. A young couple with a little son. 'Happy as ever'. So it looked. Nobody knew of the sore moments that passed between the husband

and the wife. But when the thing happened those left behind realized what they had lost. Heart attacks were unusual for that age. Almost unheard of. The young boy was insanely in love with his father. They knew he was an insanely addictive boy when he was very young. He collected white pebbles with a passion. He had an exact count of them. He knew what time father would be home. He had a strict timetable for him. Dylan was six when Aunty Mangala came to school to pick him up while the teacher got ready to introduce the letter F to a group of first graders. And while the teacher put the Winnie- the-Pooh lunch box back into the bag to send Dylan home she remembered how she had lost her own father at thirteen.

They had served Marie and Nice biscuits after the funeral. That was fun - because they had all got filled up on biscuits and for the first time since his father came home 'hurt' in a 'kuffin' he was being treated like a normal kid. He had been irritated by the way everyone was extra attentive to him. There was something creepy about that. As if they had all done something very wrong and were trying to make up for that. Dylan tugged his father's black blazer until a wailing adult dragged him away to the kitchen. So the creepy feeling continued. Until cousin Jeewaka told him that Uncle Mahesh was not just hurt. He was a lot hurt. Dead more like it, he had told Dylan matter-of-factly, with raised brows. Brows on their toes that made Uncle Mahesh dead. Dead ended with a low. Dead ended with a thud and no rhythm. Dead with hands together in the kuffin. Dead with the best suit on. Oh! So. Why hadn't anybody told him that his father was dead? Maybe he should go and ask his father about that. But everybody started bawling a little louder when he went around to see the kuffin and father in it.

Two weeks later mother made an important announcement

after the funeral. "Dylan, your thaththi won't be coming back you know."

"Why? Is it because he's dead?" Dead had no rhythm.

"Yes Dylan."

"He won't come at all?" Dead with hands together in the kuffin.

"No baby. I'm sorry."

"At all?" Dead with the best suit on.

Mother started crying. Dylan watched. Mother wept like a child. Dylan watched with blank eyes. Mother wept making horrible noises of agony which Dylan found to be creepy. They reminded him of the 'fune-rle'.

"He can't come Dylan."

"Is that why we had a fune-rle?"

"Yes, that's really why."

He understood of course. Father won't be coming home after the fune-rle.

She remarried for protection or she would have postponed she told her critical friends. She told the non-critical that this man she was to marry was a good caring one. She had her first boyfriend at sixteen. And the third lover became the first husband. She was taught in her tender years that a man always looked after the woman. And maybe it was one of those lessons that she had learnt hard. So Dylan had a late sister when he was twelve. He called her cute. Because Dylan had heard somewhere that that was what they called little babies. His mother made a few mistakes which made gaping holes in her life as time went by.

a) She never explained to Dylan why re-marriage was necessary.
b) She never understood that discipline must be backed with a genuine sense of affection.

c) She never realized that marriage was not necessarily a safety net.
d) She never made the effort to understand that re-marriage made her rather miserable.

He started beating him over a bad report card. Dylan knew even before he reached for the belt that he was going to suffer. He was going to be treated like a slave. He knew he was going to hurt cruelly. He could see the eyes working up to it. He watched, getting scared. He looked at mother. He kept looking at mother. Looking. At mother. Mother watched. Mother suffered from all forms of paralysis that moment. As if nervous. As if unaware of the cruelty about to take place. Unaware of what she could do. He hit him. Dylan screamed and jumped up in pain.

"MOTHER!"

Mother was paralyzed.

"MOTHER!"

He hugged her legs. He hit him while he hugged her legs. She watched while he hugged her legs. Discipline was important for little boys, or no telling what they would turn out to be later when they grow up. She was quaintly glad that he cared so much about her son. Dylan studied hard. But he never got good report cards, even when he studied really hard. As if the teacher knew about what happened in the household and appreciated it.

Dylan received beatings regularly from the disciplinarian-father. In retaliation early English lessons were recalled. Oliver Twist had a happy ending despite the beatings, didn't it?

"Did you get really mad the other day? Or you pretended?"
"I pretended."

"Good. I thought, maybe, you know…"

"Yeah I know. Saw your mom this morning. She looks very pretty." Kala sounded bright. Like a nine year old boy who had seen his favourite cricketer in real life.

"Yes I know."

"You don't look one bit like her."

"I know." Quiet, rusty, aged tone that carried heavy barrels of iron.

"I haven't seen your father much though. I'll bet he looks good too. And you're the odd one out!"

"Yes."

"Are you the only one in the family? I haven't seen anyone else come to church other than you and your mother and then your dad on Christmas!" Big crooked smile.

"I have a sister." Quiet, rusty aged iron barreled tone.

"Really? How old?"

"Five." Quiet rusty heavy barreled tone.

"Montessori?"

"Yes. What kind of music do you like?" And the crayons were laid down on the poster that would be put up later by two boys from the youth club from church near the big supermarket in town. And Kala's mother would come home and tell her that she was very proud of her daughter.

"Music? No."

"OK."

He looked away as she rubbed the chalk hard on the Bristol board.

Kala dreaded walking into the house. She had forgotten. Nirmaleen wouldn't understand. Nirmaleen would call her a bad sister who didn't care. Kala the bad sister, she would say. Kala would keep her head bowed while accusations hurled. Kala would be condemned and warned against bad sistering.

"You forgot."

"That's not true."

"You did."

"I didn't!"

"Because I'm blind?"

"No."

"Because I'm blind."

"No. That's a stupid suggestion."

"You forgot."

"Yes I did. I'm sorry."

"How? You're always on my mind."

"You are too." And Estrangement was trying to make a quick back-door-exit.

"Lying!"

"How was the speech?"

"You were supposed to be there." Nirmaleen breathed hard. Unpleasant loud hard gulps of breath.

Kala asked then softly, "Do you come for me? Who comes for me?"

"You never ask me."

"Remind me to ask you the next time!"

"Who's at the begging end? You or I?" Nirmaleen waited.

Kala did not reply. And then she started slowly. "You're luckier without eyes. It's easy to feel sorry for you." Then it all sounded wrong. Like some huge betrayal to the fact that she had always protected her little sister who wasn't just blind and special but unself-piteous and special. So the words 'sorry' rang the air. And the air mocked the word. As if it was a whore on the road at daytime. The sister mocked it. As if it was wrong grammar.

"I'm sorry."
"So am I." Hurt blew huge bubbles and laughed bitterly.
"But you're better than me." *Shut up Kala! Apologies are for small crimes.* And little Armies of Shame marched by respectfully with bowed heads.

A line that was precariously thin, held what was thought to be Normal and Happy. No one bothered to broaden the Normal and Happy Line, while things ran normal and happy. SNAP was cruel that way. SNAP issued no warnings of impending disaster, or of turmoil potentially unbearable. Death wasn't funny either. It was a fact that most liked to think didn't exist. So when it did rub its presence in - they all cried. They cried till eyes went red and blotchy. They cried till people came over to condole. They cried till banners came on streets expressing sympathy. They cried till others agreed that fate had been cruel. They cried a little more because it was only a young girl. Those that were the closest reminisced memories. A very common soothe technique - half way grief preserved as soothing as some termed it.

No actually I was here before you!
I just went near the wastepaper bin to sharpen my pencil Kala. Ask her, I was here before you!
Gosh! OK! You are so stuck-up! You know that!
Yeah. So?
I don't' think you know what that means! And the lips went haughty and crooked.
I don't? She bit her lip trying hard to look unshaken.
What does it mean?

Why should I tell you? Lips began to look redder.
Ha! So you don't know what it means!
Get lost! She had heard that on the cartoon she watched the evening before.
Do you get those yet?
Get what?
'That.' Eye brows on their toes expressively.
No-o. Why? Do you? Kala looked horrified.
Yes.
Really?
Head nods.
Does it hurt?
Head nods.
Did they lock you up in a room?
Head nods and the eyes roll.
Did they have a party?
Head nods and the eyes roll.
Wow!
You haven't got it?
Head shakes.
Sure? You're not lying to me? Eyes narrow threateningly.
Head shakes violently.
Tell me when you do. I think you are one of the last to be one.
Head nods and the eyes cloud, worried.

Two weeks later Kala started getting her period. But it took her one month to tell Sumanthi about it. Because she was scared that everybody would make fun of her. She hated being locked up in the room for seven days and treated like some special thing on the day they had the party. And she hardly ate any of the nice dishes they made. Mother said better avoid the oily dishes. Oily dishes, said grandmother were fatal for the tummy of a young woman who had just attained puberty. Kala learned a little later that 'Big Girl Parties' (as they were called) were common in Sri Lanka and every girl went through it unless she belonged to the super-liberal. So she consoled herself and had idealistic reveries about how she would one day become a lawyer and ban the practice.

You don't like this guy; you just have a thing for him!
Not troooo!
OK. Do whatever you want.
I will go out with him.
Congratulations! And sarcasm mounted right onto the peak and stuck a flag.

When Sumanthi broke up with Pradeep she cried. Just like any teenage girl it seemed the most practical thing to do. It would have seemed callous not to. She cried while Kala looked on with appropriate pity. Some close friends whispered how 'Sumanthi took it bad'. Sumanthi enjoyed the merit of enduring an ordeal of such a grand scale while the others looked on. Three days of complete misery. Then she started 'getting over' it. Too many guys liked her. Flattery dragged her out of misery. Some called to find out how she was. Some called to agree that Pradeep was a jerk and she never should have. She sniffed through such conversations. She liked them. She missed them when the heat of the break up died. Chocolates that Kala bought to comfort helped alleviate the misery and grow a few pimples here and there. And the myth developed that nasty break ups grew pimples. And girls from school started using pimple deterrents in the aftermath of a break up.

3

Do you think we'll be best friends forever?
Duh! Why do you bother asking? Of course! If you get a husband I'll come and drag you!
Yuck! I won't marry!
If you do.
Kala giggled. Sumi giggled harder. They had just made it to the upper school. The age of eleven was a milestone and a time to discuss important details like Forever Friendships.
Do you fancy white chocolate or brown?
Is white really chocolate?
So they say.
Sumi giggled hard. The I-know-everything-intelligent giggle. Only Sumi knew to giggle that way.
I don't think white's chocolate, Kala said confidently.
I knew you wouldn't like it.
Kala don't cry if I die.
Kala rolled eyes.
Kala will you cry if I die?

Kala rolled eyes.
Kala, what if I die?
I won't cry.
You are a hopeless brown chocolate lover.
What if Kala died? But you won't die Kala.
What if?
We'll see.
What do you mean we'll see?
We will have to see.
Kala tried hard not to slouch.
Sumi said she wanted to pee. Kala followed her to the bathroom.

Kala thought about the boy from the elocution class. The class with the elocution boy in it. The books which the elocution boy saw. The books for elocution were neat, covered in neat brown paper. He had a tiny growth, which was new to a fourteen year old. It made him look appallingly awkward like most fourteen year olds with the first signs of manhood. Kala thought it made him look unusually average. She thought he was unusually average in his elocution as well. He pronounced words with less glamour and less interest. She called him different. He wasn't. Later she deduced there was nothing attractive about the boy. The theory of averagehood began to look murky then. It was a good thing she didn't try out anything with him. There was nothing to learn together. They both knew to spell and pronounce.

Battles were always unplanned. Because there was a genuine desire for peace. But they were both compulsive in nature, and almost absently resorted to large scale bickering. There was no specific ceremony to celebrate making up, but for the next two days, heightened levels of thoughtfulness were to be expected. And there were high hopes of talking about the fights with a funny sense of pride when they were older and grown up. It wasn't everyone who made up after nasty battles, some battles went on for ages, so they had a good reason to save the battle-make-ups for the future. Perhaps to share with the newer friends they would meet later. Except when a lorry came by. Except when one was left behind. The cortège was about to leave. So Kala smoothed the black skirt she had bought in a hurry for a church function during Christmas and joined the crowd.

Kala briefly remembered that she over-paid for the skirt.

Kala what if I die?

I will roll eyes.

Kala will you cry if I die?

No. I will roll my eyes.

Kala which type of chocolate?

Brown please.

But why not white?

Please brown please.

Kala don't cry if I die.

I WON'T!

There were dolphins in the showcase. Small white ones that glittered. Sumi bought one since she knew it wouldn't violate the Animal Rule. That year was dedicated to animals. Kala had wanted to dedicate it to animals since the previous year had been for movies; animals were such a contemporary topic. They always dedicated the year for something contemporary as agreed between the two parties. So on Kala's eighteenth birthday the two of them had gone shopping and Sumi had bought a dolphin. So a ceramic dolphin for hundred and fifty rupees for Kala from Sumi with love. Kala didn't buy a toy animal or a real one. She bought the theme object for next year. They had agreed that it should be racing cars. Because they had both fallen in love with Formula One. So a blue racing car from a toyshop for Sumi with love on her birthday. Sumi complained and expressed concern over the lawlessness, but accepted the gift, nonetheless. Kala decided later that it was an indication of an unnatural premature occurrence to come. She should have known that rules were too sacred to be broken.

Urban Sri Lanka was a difficult mix. There were the ruthless Conservatives that expected nineteenth century morals to return with a vengeance. Those who were at the other extreme, thought that it was lack of opportunity that created the freaks called Conservatives. The Middlers were unbelievably shrewd; moral stance entirely dependent on associations with acquaintances from the two extremes. The Ultra Modern were the few the Conservatives termed American-Wannabes who tried to challenge the ethics embedded in a strongly cultural Buddhist society. It was a sad mix for a country that desperately tried to push up its Growth Indicators.

It was too late now, rules had been broken and prices paid in large sums never agreed upon. Kala never forgot about birthday cards that soaked the paper with water colours. SNAP! All plans for the next decade would take a reverse turn. They had plans to exasperate the future husbands and divorce them. They had plans to become music stars one day, winning an award for their music. Sumi had argued that acting in movies would be easier and winning awards would be easy since they could act more compulsive than Sangeetha. The argument had been left unsettled. And then SNAP trotted by. As if welcome. As if casual. As if no harm. As if undramatic. As if mundane. SNAPping life out of the best friend was an unforgivable crime. Didn't SNAP know that? SNAP couldn't know. SNAP didn't know. BUT SNAP SHOULD HAVE! SNAP BLOODY SHOULD HAVE.

Caller 1
"How are you Kala?"
"OK."
"How are things?"
"OK."
"You must learn to move on. I understand that it must be traumatic, but you must try to forget about it."
"OK."
"I know you must be still in shock, after seeing your best friend knocked down."
"Yes, the vegetable lady is here, can I call you back?"

Caller 13
"How are things? Are you better now"?
"OK."
"It must have been awful, seeing it with your eyes."
"It was."
"But you must be strong now, you have exams after all."
"There's a rat in my room I think. Can I call you back?"

Kala's diary: June 3rd
Written three days after the funeral. Eight days after they had

gone shopping for blue T-shirts for an event in school where they were supposed to appear as Car-Wash girls for a play! A couple of hundred hours since a Tata Lorry on the pedestrian crossing in front of the school had knocked down Sumanthi. Kala had stood on the other side of the crossing watching as people clustered to find out what happened. She had held her breath and watched. There was no point in cutting classes the next day to go blue-socks-shopping. She would have to go to Sumi's place. Preferably in black and white.

And so the diary:

If there are ugly little surprises all over the place, this is the ugliest. How does the mind begin to repair this mess? Lorries. Ugly bloody Lorries. Life will never be the same will it? How does it return to normal when there is nothing normal to return to? I can't think straight anymore. I can only cry. Watch funeral handbills taking their places on numerous weather beaten walls and buildings. Numerous feet walking in and out of the house in various whites. Various who think they should talk to me. Sumi's gone Diary. SNAP! Gone. Deepest sympathies? How are you? Fuck off. She's not coming back.

"Aunty?"
"Who's calling?"
"Kala."
"Kala dear, Sumi hasn't come yet."
"Yes. I know. A lorry on the crossing near school knocked down your daughter. She's dead. I'm sorry." And she hung up on the screaming mother. Who wanted to listen to a screaming mother anyway? At the funeral Kala noticed that Sumi's mother had a

persistent cough.

Caller 23
"How are you holding up?"
"OK."
"How's school stuff?"
"OK."
"How's Sumi's mother?"
"Bad. She might die one of these days."
"That bad?"
"Yes. She lost her daughter."
"OK then maybe I'll talk to you later Kala."
"OK."

Caller 31
"Kala, I'm sorry about your friend."
"Thank you Dylan. So am I."
"How are you?"
"Why do you ask? You know sympathy can be unbearable sometimes."
"I hope you don't think I'm sympathizing."
"What are you doing then?"
"Being your friend."
"Thank you. We'll do this being my friend thing some other time."

Three months after the accident Kala tried to figure out what the salient features of a market economy were. Kala didn't know about market economies. Market economies were good for those with living friends. Market economies were perilous for those

who had dead, knocked-down friends. What were the provisions in the Shop and Office Act that protected women? Her friend got knocked down by a lorry not too long ago. But she wrote. Because she promised mother that she won't let things get in the way. Promises were important. Sumi never broke promises.
"So you passed."
"Yes I passed A/Levels. I planned to pass too."
"I was so sure you planned to fail," Dylan teased lightly, as if he was used to light teasing.
"Why?"
"That was sarcasm."
"Sarcasm?" As if she had never heard the word before.
"I was joking."
"Oh. Buy me ice cream?"
"Why?"
"I passed exams. I deserve ice cream," Kala said in a tone of Cleopatra importance.
"Hold my hand then?"
"No!"
"Why?"
"That would seem," she shrugged confidentially, "you know," shrugged again, "odd."
"Oh! But you won't get ice cream then." Dylan raised his eyebrows waiting like the colonel who launches an attack on the enemy and waits for the sound of victory and the opponent's cries of retreat.
"I'll buy ice cream for myself. Thank you. You can't blackmail me!"
His face fell then. Dylan looked sad. Dylan looked like a little boy spanked in public - not just public, but a little-

girl-public. Kala held his hand. "Ice cream for me please?"

In the days to come Estrangement would be sorely missed for the dormancy it offered. Even grief would seem acceptable. The end of the non-bubble era. Bubbles hurt when they grew bigger. Bubbles came unannounced too, just like Estrangement.

The Beginning of the Tree House Movie

The Tree House movie started right after the Blup Shampoo commercial. Shampoo for everyday use. The Daily Hair Booster. Dylan used soap. Since he was yet to discover Metrosexual Fads. It simply appeared as *The Tree House* against a thick black backdrop. Then in smaller characters appeared 'starring Batty Baxter' Dylan the number one Batty Baxter fan was nailed to the chair. Dylan watched with haunted pupils. The Tree House movie was neat. Sassy. Laughed a lot. Ate a lot. Belched a lot. Yawned. Climbed trees and made houses up there. Dylan watched dazed, dumb.
"Dad, this is so cool."
"Well, you're my son," said Batty Baxter as he hugged the son.
The Tree House was large. Striking. And more importantly involved a Responsible Father.
"Careful, watch your step." To the son.
"Don't worry dad, I'm OK." To the dad.
Dylan watched dazed, dumb. As the credits rolled on at the end of the movie, Dylan made several crucial decisions.
1) I will make a similar Tree House movie.
2) I will make a striking Tree House.
3) I will dedicate the Tree House to a special person in my life called Father.
Dylan researched fanatically on Tree Houses over the next few

weeks. He found out that most kids at school knew about them, or at least pretended to. He found out that most parents were not for Tree Houses, consequently they were against them. He tried to find out why. It appeared that Tree Houses were high, and kids could fall off them. Then came the jackpot of his search quest. There was a kid in class who actually had a Tree House. A boy with a Tree House. A real one that Dylan could visit. Dylan made quick plans. He dropped the boy's crayons cleverly all over the place. Then he helped pick them up. He made conversation. He asked questions that seemed very pertinent.

"Who made the Tree House for you?

"My brother did."

"Is it, uh, big?"

"Yeah, sort of." He nodded like it wasn't a big deal. He had a huge accent. Dylan hated that. Dylan tried to take it in. His heart raced like a racer bike. A real Tree House!

The next week at the kid's birthday, Dylan chose a chair by the Tree House and sat there till mother came to pick him up.

"Do you think it's really difficult to feel happy?"

"Maybe. When did you last feel happy Kala?"

"Now."

"You feel happy now?" he asked pointedly squinting his eyes.

"Yes" she looked at him, waiting for an assault. He was going to say she didn't know what happiness was, stupid fool. She shouldn't have brought up the issue with him. "Yes" she said. Louder, just to reinforce, just in case assault became ugly and brutal. She didn't trust him. "Of course." She nodded her head again.

"So, what's the purpose of that earlier question?"

"Which one?"

"You don't even remember what you asked? Are you *that* happy?" he asked squinting his eyes again. Dylan the Eye-Squinter.

"What did I ask?"

"You have a beautiful smile." She smiled.

"Are you happy now?"

The smile disappeared. "I didn't mean flattery."

"If it could make you happy?"

"It didn't. What if they sold happiness in shops?"

He smiled. Sympathetically she thought. She started stubbing the pebbles in the church garden. They were pretty too, without dense brains like Dylan, Dylan couldn't even think happiness was shoppable.

"They don't." Dylan said softly. Eyes squinted still.

"I wish they did."

"May be they will. In packets!" He laughed and brushed back his hair.

"In packets. Packets with smiley faces on them!"

"Packets with Tree Houses on them!" he said laughing.

"Tree houses?"

He shook his head and continued laughing. Kala watched a little girl walk into church. Then suddenly Kala started laughing. The way she used to laugh when she was small and saw Shaggy from Scooby Dooby Doo looked freaked out on TV. She always found his freaked out face funny.

"Do you hide things Kala?"

"Like what?"

"Things you think are odd to talk about in the open."

"You mean stuff like underwear?" and she looked serious.

"No. Not stuff like underwear. Stuff like how you feel about people because you don't want to sound odd."

"Stuff like whether I'm still grieving?"

"Are you still grieving?" he asked gently, curiously wanting to hug her. Hug his friend? *Would she mind? Aye, she would.*

"Yes. I always will."

Kala's diary: February 4th (Independence Day)

Independence Day was when everyone got a holiday to celebrate the independence won by forefathers in 1948. National flags were put up and special messages were issued by the President, the Prime Minister and other dignitaries. And the people imbibed everything without showing any sarcasm. Who was going to capture the average-citizen-sarcasm anyway on television?

So the diary on Independence Day:

This is crazy, how happy I am when I'm with you, talking about nothing. They make no sense. Mostly stuff, but the importance they hold in conversations. Isn't that weird? As if what you thought mattered? About pencils. About shirts. About songs. About a pimple on the nose. About a nail that is broken. About ice cream that didn't taste good. About going here. About dropping in there. And I'm happy filling time with nothing. I miss that – the very moment you're gone. And then I wonder who drives this powerful impact on me? On all levels of sanity? Who makes it so easy for me to toss all my emotions on you – as if it were safe? It's harrowing then – because SNAP has taught me not to be too playful with fate. SNAP is a harsh disciplinarian. Maybe I should stop about nothings. They are too important, a little too connected to the core levels of sanity. SNAP will be incensed.

"Imagine, it would be so easy if you could see my mind."
"Why?"
"I don't have to waste my breath."
"True."
"But it would be difficult for those who cannot read well."
"You are kidding me! You can't read!"
"No!"
"Oh shit!" She looked unbelieving, but considered the possibility already.
"Yeah." Big Superman cheeky smile.
"But you talk OK Dylan."
"Hmmm…but don't read OK." He looked somber. The Unreading somber Dylan next to the Condescending literate Kala.
"How come?" asked the Literate Kala.
"Never found out," said the Somber Unreading Dylan.
"I think it's called something. You could have got help for that." said Literate Kala the Philanthropist.
"Really? Gee! I didn't know!"
"I don't believe you!"
"You can't read the mind at all."
"So you were lying?"
"Yes."
"So you can read?"
"Not the mind. But really I meant it. Think, it would be simple if people could read the mind. Stuff like honesty would mean no big deal. Everything would be so uncomplicated."
"You want someone to read your mind? Or are you having a tough time being an honest kid?"
"Something like that. Look, need to go home. I'll see you around?"

"Sure thing. And maybe you could help me with my reading problem?"
Kala thought he laughed like a cartoon monster. A very wicked one. She raised her middle finger.

The Continuation of the Tree House Movie and Related Matters

If father had been not-dead, Tree House making would require getting up early. Dylan would beg for five minutes longer in bed and father would come and drag him out of bed. If father had been not-dead. If the movie were to be of course. Ifthemovieweretobe. There would be equipment like ladders, ropes and planks. There would be a tricky nail box that would fail to budge, Ifthemovieweretobe. There would be a big dog like Larry J in the movie, that could pounce it open. Dylan worried. There was no dog at home. There was no father at home. But he could borrow Ringo for a day? Ringo could crash into it. Ifthemovieweretobe.

There were planks in the shed, after last year's shed making. *Dad, this is so cool.* There was a huge nail box, just like in the movie. Dylan sighed in relief. One less thing to worry about. He needed to figure out where the keys to the shed were.
"I need the keys to the shed."
"Why Dylan?" Mother sharp. Mother always sharp.
"I have my old boots there." Dylan the tactless liar.
"Please don't take them out and dirty the place."
Please, I badly need the keys.
"I have some old scrap books where I've pasted some pictures that I need for my school work." Dylan swallows and breathes hard.
"What school work?"

"History." Dylan doesn't flinch. Dylan the tactful liar.
"What pictures?"
"Pictures of Kings."
"And they are in the shed? They are *all* in the shed?"
"No, just eight kings."
Mother stares at Dylan balefully. Dylan, the calm casual liar, waiting.
"Eight kings are in the shed?"
"Yes, in my old scrap book."
"OK. Give me the keys back in two minutes." Mother lifts two food-moist fingers to indicate two. Like two minutes.

He cried out most of the time, not only because it hurt. But because it was humiliating to be beaten by the stepfather while boys in his class were improving on their macho skills. But he was only intense in looks. Not the physique. He was no match against the stepfather. So when he went to school with bruises, on some days he said his family had gone to the beach the previous day and the bruises came from beach rugby. Some who were still very childish at fifteen and needed to acquire intelligence bought his story, but there were the others who were skeptical. There were the skepti-sympathetic and the skepti-scornful. So Dylan had friends, but not many. By eighteen, beatings reduced considerably. And Dylan gained self-esteem. His first girlfriend was Lakshi. Pretty. Not smart. Pretty with a huge bum. Pretty Lakshi with a huge bum with lots of things to say. Pretty Lakshi who wore smart pants to show off the huge bum. She asked him on Day Three when they went to a fast food outlet whether he loved her.
"Of course. Why do you ask?" he said.

She smiled back shyly. Red and shy. Lots of things to tell her girlfriends. But two weeks later Dylan said maybe things shouldn't get complicated.

"Why do you think things are complicated?"

"They are."

"They aren't."

"I want to break up."

"Oh!" Then lots of things to tell Lakshi's girlfriends. Bastard.

But Bastard was such a temporary tag. Nobody complained when the bastard asked out. It was the ultimate moment of compassion. Or the jealous called it the ultimate moment of flattery. Compassion reigned. Flattery smirked. As if the bastard had changed. As if the bastard was no more. Nadia. Flirted back generously.

"They say you are a bastard."

"And they say you are a bitch."

"They say you get bored with your girlfriends."

"They say you behave like Cleopatra around Caesar."

"How did you become a bastard?"

"The same way you became a bitch."

"I don't like them."

"Nor do I."

"But I like you."

"And I like you more for that."

Nadia drove a Beetle. Nadia lasted longer. Nadia got drunk and demanded sex. Dylan laughed it off sheepishly thinking it was a ruse.

"Ruse? Where did you learn that?"

"From a comic strip."

"This is real life. And sex is no ruse."
Nadia taught things that she knew. She told him that being teenagers was about radical fun that will leave room for regret if it were that, but there was no point in thinking about that now. Now was the time to enjoy, because there was nothing like enjoyment.
"And so this is enjoyment?"
"Yes. Lovely ain't it?"
Nadia lasted exactly one year and two weeks. Within that time Dylan became unwittingly monogamous. During the same time Nadia became unwittingly monogamous.
"I hear you ain't seeing anyone else."
"I hear the same puritanical shit about you."
"Do you have a problem with it?"
"Yes."
"So do I. Start cheating on me."
"By all means."
And after two weeks she declared she needed out.
"Why?"
"Because you are cheating on me."
He raised his eyebrows.
"Bastard."

Paper shredding came to be something like a soul-searching exercise that gave self-control and recuperated sense. He loved it. There was something soothing about shredding it to bits as it became powerless to stand its ground and struggled against the softest of the breeze. He never depended on anyone. Not his mother after the blue-satin-shirt-ceremony. Not his father since he died. And nobody thereafter. Paper shredding broke the world into bits and gave him control.

"Did you come to see me?"

"No."

"Then why?"

"Because church is where people pray."

"I wish you had come to see me and this wasn't an accidental meeting."

Kala laughed. But she was flattered. She wanted to ask. To be blunt and ask why he said that, but she didn't.

"You have a high pitched voice."

"No I don't." And that came in a decidedly flat, low-pitched tone.

"Not now."

"Then when?"

"Just a couple of minutes back."

She shrugged defensively. Dylan was an eternal attacker. She needed to be cautious around him. Even the pitch of the voice needed to be monitored. Suddenly she felt self-conscious. She bit her lips, thinking perhaps they were a little paler than usual. He might think she had pale lips. Her head felt as if drenched in coconut oil and she wondered whether this was how it happened. Was this how it happened?

"Do you kill mosquitoes?" he asked looking around as if discussing a state secret.

"That's a duh question, isn't it?" She made a face.

"Is it?"

"What's so important about killing mosquitoes?" She made another face, but returned to normal, worried that perhaps it made her look ugly.

"There's nothing important, but it's not duh Kala - just coz you ask about stuff like reading the mind, there's nothing dumb about asking whether you kill mosquitoes! This is as bad as you saying sop is poppy!"

So she started laughing - *sop is poppy!* "That's cute," She said between giggles. Of course he laughed too. It was his gag after all. This probably wasn't how it happened. People falling in love didn't giggle, right? Yes, there had to be another way, this probably wasn't how it happened.

"Yeah I kill mosquitoes, so?"

"Good. They are a pain. I'm allergic to them."

He showed off dark spots on his arms.

Mosquitoes were small and evil looking. Love would have chosen a softer route for expression. Kala was relieved. And she had held her breath too thinking that this was how it happened!

Estranged Case 3: Nadia

Nadia started reading at an early age. She read while the mother complained about lack of order in the house due to such arduous reading tendencies. Father didn't. Father thought it was very good. She read *Tom Thumb* alone. Even the *Twelve Dancing Princesses* alone. She even began reading grown up novels at home when only Nishanthi the helper in the house was there. They told her tales of thirty-something women breaking free. From husbands, from harrowing jobs, from countries of deprivation. Father became daddy. Like in the books. It was perfectly acceptable for the super rich to adopt western terms of endearment. Father didn't think it was odd either. He responded either way. Mother was mostly without salutation. Just the barest words. Mother ran a salon for the super wealthy that reported huge profits every year and father ran a software company that had a passion to meet deadlines. He always met deadlines as she gathered from conversations that contained pride, capacity and bargaining power. Nishanthi was the helper who helped. She cooked food. She washed Nadia baba's clothes. She combed Nadia baba's hair. She located Nadia baba's lost accessories. Lost shoes. Lost clothes. So estrangement started slowly and almost nervously but soon gained pace. Nobody bothered with estrangement. Not even the super rich who should have had time to worry about their only child. But it didn't have meaning where salons were glamour and deadlines were a passion. Daddy's company had made huge profits for the last six years in a row. On Nadia's eighteenth birthday, came the ultimate expression of love. A Beetle. Quite a high on a birthday. Nobody spoke about PAYE implications of such. That was considered a tad out of fashion.

Nadia started 'seeing someone' as it was termed, at twelve. At the time 'seeing someone' was daring and new. It was a big deal even to know someone who 'saw' someone. She had to be daring. She was rich. The rich condoned that behaviour. As some put it, they could afford it. And some of the more reasonable minded asked what there was to afford anyway? She two-timed. Three-timed. Before she could fall in love with anyone she 'saw' that he did something that made her feel infinitely superior to him. She always felt invulnerable around her multi-dates. By eighteen, things were established. The conventional disapproved of her. Her past dates called her 'a tart' with a vengeance. She received comments with amusement. Nadia didn't mind what the emotionally unchallenged thought. She almost loved the scandal she created. They didn't hold high rankings in her book either. They were what they were. Too scared to break free and vented out their frustration on free souls like her. She pitied them enormously for that.

On Tree-House Making -
Tensions and what happened after 'that'

There were eight planks lying on one another near the tree. The tree. The tree that would be in Ifthemovieweretobe. The tree was a grown mango tree with a bear seat to rest the house. Dylan could easily climb to the seat of the tree, and start building the base of it. And then it came in a rush. It all came in a confused rush. They used special types of cameras up in Tree Houses. There were too many technicalities. How in the world was he going to find out what they called those cameras? Does he write to the TV station? Nope Nopie Nope. Ask mother? How would he ask her? Mother what do you call camera like lenses that they use to see far? No. She wouldn't care. Mother wouldn't know. Mother was dumb. Ifthemovieweretobe couldn't go on without removing constraints. Ask mother.

4

"Why do you like colours?"
"I like them."
"What do you like about them? And don't give me dumb explanations!" Kala waited with widened pupils. Waiting for a smart answer. Dylan looked worried. As if this was a task he couldn't handle. Then he snapped out of it, feeling smarter than ever.
"OK. Then don't ask," he said cockily like Superman.
"I hoped to find a brain in there." Kala tried to sound like a disappointed judge at a ballet competition.
"You hoped wrong."
"My mistake." Thin smile and toying fingers that looked very busy suddenly. Toying became a vexing process that required energy.
"OK let's see Kala … I have a lot of reasons for liking colours. I like them because they are how I remember my childhood. My father died when I was six."
"I'm sorry. Dylan. I had no idea."
"That's an ugly word you know."
"Sorry, I won't say sorry again."
"You could shut up and still mean a lot."

She pursed her lips tight and squinted her eyes.

He grinned. "I remember colours with him. I don't even know why. That's how it is. Whenever I close my eyes to remember him I remember colours. Especially blue!"

"You like blue?" she asked excited.

"Yes. But why is blue spelled with an E at the end? Why couldn't it be B-L-U?"

"I don't know."

"Even yellow. It could be just Y-E-L-L-O right?"

"Absolutely."

"Kala do you think you'll go out with me?"

"No." She waited and then started again. "Because you see, you and I are good friends." Thin smile and toying fingers that looked busy.

"Friends shouldn't go out? No? Why?"

"Friends are better than lovers."

"Says who?"

"I do."

"OK. Then we shouldn't. But I still think it'll be lots fun."

"Really?"

"Hmmm."

"I find it a bit complicated."

"Why?"

"Lovers kiss, don't they?"

"Yeah. What's wrong with that?"

"I don't like kissing. There's something pathetic about it."

"You like it. You just don't want to admit it. You're too shy!"

He sounded cocky, like Superman.

"No I'm not."

"OK."

"And lovers put their arms around each other and get very soppy no?"

"Yes Kala."

"I don't like that."

"If you have any other suggestions on how lovers can express themselves to one another I don't mind helping you try them out."

"No. I don't support the idea of going out anyway."

Dylan had been almost different. He hardly spoke about himself.

"Omigosh Dylan," Nadia loud and bouncy in her hello. And Dylan would repeat in a decidedly lower pitch. "Omigosh Nadia." He kissed passionately. Excitedly. As if this was his lifeline. She felt quaint and dizzy every time he did. But she always brushed it away thinking it didn't matter. Sometimes in her very imaginative moods she wondered whether his silence had been cold or warm. Cold? Had it been because he couldn't be bothered with conversation? Warm? Had it been because he loved to hear her talk so much that he listened? Whatever it had been, silence had been attractive. Nadia taught him things that he had been willing to learn. She told him that no matter what women said they really couldn't help feeling flattered over compliments. She told him that women got bored with poor attempts at humour, and consequently wouldn't find the guy all that attractive. She told him that virginity was a label for those who dreamt of a happy marriage later. And virginity was supposed to add to the happiness and solidity in marriage. So they were restraining themselves in their teenage years. She told him that she didn't believe in marriage because every one of those knots boiled down to an em-

barrassing social condition at some point. She also told him that women spent hours before the mirror, not because they wanted to impress any bloke, but because they had a natural inferiority complex that took great pains in trying to enhance facial beauty. She told him other things. Things that she judged he would understand with perfect composure unlike most freaks she had met before. She said all women thought of themselves as potential models before the mirror. And then Dylan had asked a single question - What did enhance mean?
Something like improve.
Thanks.

When Kala started working as a banking assistant, her mother was very happy for her. She had always worried whether Kala would move on properly after Sumanthi's death. And with the job it seemed like she had something to concentrate on other than lost friends. Estrangement continued nonetheless. Walked miles in Kala's head and introduced her to late entrants like Bubbles.

Kala's mother was closer to her than she was to the mother. The mother still had no idea that estrangement was a very sad story that locked up sweet relationships and made emotional zombies of those capable of lovely feelings. So she was happy, and she was a loving mother who worried about the normal things that worried all mothers who had nineteen-year-old daughters. She worried whether Kala would find an unsuitable man. She worried about Kala's health. She worried about Kala's looks. She worried about Kala's safety on the road, especially after Sumanthi. And when she went to church on Sunday she prayed to God to keep her daughters safe. Especially her nineteen year old who was shy, backward and quiet and just trying on her wings.

Dinner with Nishanthi: Nadia had dinner with Nishanthi on rare nights that she didn't go out. Dinner with Nishanthi had its humorous aspects. Nishanthi worried about Nadia's health. Nishanthi worried about her looks. Nishanthi worried about her safety in the Beetle alone, especially with all the road accidents that the papers reported. She also worried about all the unsuitable men she knew Nadia hung out with. Nadia exasperated her further by mentioning their names at dinner.

Dinner with Parents: had its good days and the bad days. Dinner was good when parents were making good business and bad when parents were not making good business. Business and its moods had a direct impact on dinner conversation. There was conversation on Nadia's studies. Nadia's future. Nadia's higher education in England. Nadia's emotional growth? What was that again? No, no, not that really. Just light teasing maybe about a boy or something. Besides what could parents ask about emotional growth? Children these days were so advanced.

Kala's diary: March 27th

You have proven things that up to now have remained myths in my mind. For example, you have proven that I am capable of thinking about a guy without really taking long breaks. Not even small ones. Then, you have proven that I'm not in love with average-hood. Because you are not average. And you have proven that I'm capable of being embarrassingly honest with people (namely you). Also you have proven that I'm perfectly capable of talking to myself (not really myself, just this wild impression in my head that you are right there next to me, and so I'm not talking to myself really. I'm talking to you). Do you think this psychotic nature will play itself down if I tell you how I feel? I have considered the possibility, but there are issues. For example - my ego is at stake. Then, the fact that I have bluffed up to now that friends are better than lovers, I still believe that, but with you it's very difficult to live up to that belief.

Kala's diary: March 28th
This is all very confusing you know. This whole shit bag of being in love or coming very close to that. As if there are no important things in the world anymore - like the fact that Myanmar is still to acquire democracy or the fact that the Spanish troops are going to pull out of Iraq. Or the fact that Sri Lanka plans to win the vote of being the best bickerers in the world. The mind is saturated. So sad. This love shit is really no fun. I have become very giddy. It's sad, because you are not even a nice guy. There's not a single thing about you that is average. So this doesn't really make sense you know? This whole shit bag I mean, about my claim that I'm in love?

Kala's diary: March 29th
I probably don't like you - I got jealous today when you mentioned Nadia, when I have no legitimate right to be so. My shit line prevents that -

> *Friends are better than lovers!*
> *Friends are better than lovers!*
> *Friends are better than lovers!*

So I got jealous and then decided that it's natural even for a friendship and then I decided that this whole shit bag about being in love will wear off, and I can pull my act together and try not to talk to myself like I'm mad.

Nadia loved fantasizing about suicide. In fact she had dreamed of being a media sensation over it. They loved to make soppy literature out of a premature death. Maybe she stood a chance? She was pretty. Smart. Rich. And young. But there were other concerns. Like the fact that maybe her parents might not be able to go through the loss.

But emotional emptiness was a sad malady. It killed happiness and encouraged suicide. As if it was a good thing. There was nothing funny about emotional emptiness-- as if there was some hollow that kept her from being happy. As if the only things that perked her up were the night-outs and the sex. Sex was hungry and inexpressive. And they didn't work on her emotional hollow. So craving for suicide. Served with pills. Served with jumping off a height. Served with anything that killed. Then she remembered. God! No! Nishanthi! Nishanthi would be thrown out if she killed herself. Where could Nishanthi go? Poor Nishanthi.

"Dylan maybe you should do something you like?"
"Like?"
"Like something you like. You know?"
"Like what?"
"What makes you happy?"
"Is that a question?"

"OK, it is."

"I really don't know. It's a tough question."

"Why?"

"It's complicated you know."

"No it's not. Just remember the times you have been really happy. Or you laughed a lot or something like that."

"OK. Is that how you find out whether someone's happy? Laugh or something?"

"Not really. I'm just trying to help you out with this."

"With what?"

Gosh! You are so un-bloody-believable!

"Like what makes you happy."

"Is that a question?" and then he noticed the exasperation. "I think I like the guitar."

"The guitar?"

"Yep that's it. The guitar."

"OK. So do you know how to play it?

"Not really. No scratch that. I don't think I really like that."

"Huh?"

"I don't like the guitar."

"All right?" She rolled her eyes right in his face. Her pupils looked exasperated.

"I don't like that. It just seemed like the type of thing that makes you happy. You know? Guitar, calm and stuff - you know?"

"I know."

"But there are things that make you happy that don't have any connection to anything. You can't define them or capture them to find out where they come from." Dylan looked and waited for a reply, as if he said something stupid and now wanted reassurance. She started laughing. Really loud, as if she remembered something stupid from a TV comedy. Then she asked almost casually, like it didn't matter. "Do you miss things?"

"Like what?"

"Childhood?" As if it only just occurred to her.

"Yes. Everyone does."

"You mean everyone does and they just don't make a big deal out of it?"

"Hmmm."

"So everyone misses it and thinks about it?"

"I think about it."

"A lot?"

"Yes."

"Like twenty-four-seven?"

"Hmmm."

"I miss it too."

"You miss school?"

"Hmmm."

"I miss it too Kala."

"But I like my life now. It's different. No real boundaries. I like it that way - but there's something wrong you know?" Then she looked at him as if desperately looking for approval.

"I know. Like you miss your growing-up buddies." He nodded.

"Can I ask a question?"

"What's new about that?"

"No. This one's awkward."

"Uh. All your questions are pretty much that."

"No. This one's awkward."

"What could be really awkward for you Kala? Anyway you ask so many awkward questions."

"No. This one's awkward."

"Ask."

"All right. But it's a bit awkward."

"I *know* that bit."

"All right. But this is just something I meant to ask. But you can always skip OK?"

"OK."

"No pressure. OK?"

"OK."

Am I going bloody nuts? "I'm actually in a brutally honest mood. OK?"

"I'm getting a bit tired of your preview shit."

"Do you like me?" All of Kala's Senses bit nails and perspired nervously. And blamed Kala for locking them out. And he stared back. She looked down at ugly feet. Complete moment of despair, ugly feet were consoling then. "Touché. Dumb question."

And the Senses nodded their heads in approval and started squirming. This was bloody embarrassing. The Senses made plans to disown her in a secret ceremony.

"Not really."

"Yeah whatever. I need to get going. I'm supposed to help Nirmaleen with an essay."

"Yes."

"I'll catch you later?"

"What I meant was - well yes. I kind of like you."

"Good. I was curious."

"That was it?"

"No. Do you like water-colour paintings?"

"Yes."

✻

Kala's diary: April 13th
Sinhala and Tamil New Year. Big occasion here when those working in the city went to their hometown packed with gifts. Blissful day when Sri Lanka went mad in a happy way.

I can't concentrate on anything anymore. I can easily call myself a psychopath now. Just that I sound very sane in public. But how can I not be one, when I cannot shut you out of my mind for even a span of three minutes at a stretch? Maybe if I used a timer I could improve on the number of minutes that my mind is free of you? Oh shit! I hate falling for you! You are such a pathetic jerk who pretends to be a nice boy at church.

There were really no crimes that the mind perceived. Crimes were robbery, terrorism, murder, rape. The mind perceived no crimes on women. The mind saw them as women. Interesting. Powerful. Tractable. Easily boring. Women laughed nervously, wanted attention and hung about wanting more each time something good came about. There was no genuine gratitude. There was no natural sensitivity that took pains to prevent cruelty. Only delicate gestures to look delicate and gentle. They didn't touch the heart. They made no sense to him. No crime in breaking hearts that wanted attention. No crime in leaving when they laughed a little too loud, or became a little too shy. He didn't particularly crave for women's attention. He just got it and didn't flatter himself over it. Women couldn't fill hollows. Their fingers were always uncertain. Too rough to touch the heart. Only Psalms could. Psalms were the best link to his childhood. Before the funeral. Psalms made him cry because they were first read when things had been happy. He remembered happy things with happy people. Kala. Pretty smile. Beautiful smile. Shy smile. Shy pretty smile. Kala. Interesting. Powerful. Tractable. Easily boring. Father died in the Kuffin. Mother married. Again. Blue Bloody Satin Shirts. Blue Fucking Satin Shirts. Father II moved in. Mother let him hit. Mother the coward. Mother didn't love him. Father II hated him. Fucking kuffins.

How did the blind fall in love? Kala wondered whether things were somehow less complicated because seeing him made it a little worse to resolve that she could get over him. She would have asked Nirmaleen, but Nirmaleen was a kid - still sixteen. She couldn't be in love this soon. And Kala had a mad enough crush on the boy from the elocution class at fourteen, but a mad crush and love were different. The blind probably found it easier.

"How are you?"
"Good. Missed me?"
Shrug "Maybe. Maybe not. Why? Does it matter?"
"No," she laughed and hugged him.
"Maybe I did."
"What's new?"
"A woman."
"Who? Married? Name?"
"The name's not important."
"Of course it is. It gives a platform to build her character."
"Kala."
"OK."
"Pretty. A little difficult to get."
"What does that mean?"

"I like her."

"Better than you liked me?"

"Hmmm."

"Bastard!" She laughed. "You asked her out?"

"My usual thing. I think she wants some romantic ceremony for that," and he started laughing. She did too. And wondered why she did.

"Why did you laugh Dylan?"

"Why did you laugh with me?"

"Contagious I think."

"I could like her."

"She sounds one of them."

"No. But she's funny."

"Does she have everything you look for?"

"And that means I'm so drawn to her physically." He rolled his eyes.

"What? Are you not?"

"I am."

"What do you like about women?"

(Shrug) "What everyone else likes. Boobs. Ass. Face. And a great sense of humour."

"That can't be what you liked about me!"

"No?"

"No."

"Yes."

"Really?"

"Hmmm. You are quite different from other women."

"I know."

"But you see. I liked you for everything that everyone else liked you for."

"That's a terrible thing to say! And I was really flattering myself." She started laughing. Then he started laughing too. She laughed casually. Asifitdidntmatter. He joined almost as if agreeing to laugh at all the things she laughed at. So it ended in laughter.

When Nadia went home she thought about it. And thought about how things had turned out. And decided that words were impermanent. Impermanent words were sad; they exposed the stupid weakling in a man. That was really sad because some people always claimed that they were One-Word people - then how the hell was the Short Term Word Syndrome to be explained?
Nadia I think you are an ek-ceptionle woman. Nadia the most ek-ceptionle woman known in the history of the earth. Nadia *I haven't met a girl like you*, followed by one of those earth-terorrizingly heavy sighs and *I don't think I will either ever again.*

Perfection built in little by little. Perfection bricks one upon the other. With One Word Cement holding them. Nadia's Castle of Perfection.

Nadia thank you for showing a side of me that I thought didn't exist. I would ne-ver leave you.

Nadia's Castle of Perfection becoming bigger everyday. Nadia watching with careless hands on the hips. Asifitdidntmatter. This castle. The Castle of Perfection. Nadia didn't live for perfection. And the bricks kept lying over with the best cement they knew. Nadia watching with careless hands on the hips. And it didntmatter at all. And even if it did it was the work of One Word People. They didn't change. And then it came. Nobody knew about it. It was like famine in a country with no assets. Nobody noticed. Brick by brick. Sturdy brick by sturdy brick. And then it came. The Castle of Perfection caught a modern type of syphilis. It smothered the bricks and liquidated the cement. They called it the Short Term Word Syndrome. And said it was nothing. Only a few Short Term Words hereandthere. Just a bit of patch up and the Order of Life would restore. Nadia would be Nadia again. (Of course.)

Short Term Word Syndrome –Phase I

The Short Term Word Syndrome rules were formed in the days when it was an item, when the sky was dark and gloomy. Sky being gloomy and dark didn't really bother anyone, because it was rather stimulating in a dark sort of way. Then what was to be formed into the Short Term Word syndrome took its course.
Ifyouweren'tsopretty I wouldn't have gone out with you!
What? And the bricks of Perfection gave away to the pressure.
Ifyouweren'tsopretty.
And if I weren't? And the bricks of Perfection gave way to the pressure.
He touched her ear and smiled crookedly. Nadia looked closely. Brick pieces gathered themselves shamefully and ran away and away.
Don't think me gorgeous, bastard?
Beautiful!
Breathtaking!

And then the Bullshit Department revealed itself. The Bullshit Department with deceiving clerks who now sniggered at the Delusional Miss Nadia! Papers would carry headlines claiming Bullshit Departments were established to break delusion to pieces such as the Castle of Perfection. Some genuinely thought that Bullshit Departments were a Good Thing playing undercover in cozy big dens.

COVER BLOWN FOR BULLSHIT DEPARTMENT
(Picture of the Castle of Perfection)

The Short Term Word Syndrome revealed freckles that had not been there all this time. Tiny scratch marks that had been ignored. The breasts that had seemed beautiful. Popularity that had been tangible. The face-shape that was thought to be perfect all this time. The Short Term Word Syndrome dug deeper and spaded out things. They were to be called things since there was no way to know what they were.

Short Term Word Syndrome-Phase II

The sky was relatively less gloomy, with signs of increasing splendour. But these were the times when the next phase of the Short Term Word Syndrome was being incubated. So such detailed skies didn't count.

Idon'tthinkyou'recapableoflove.

Dylan laughed himself into hysteria.

Nadia pouted comically.

Idon'tthinkyou'recapableoflove.

Dylan doubled over.

And who said I was? He asked finally recovering.

A guy like you cannot care. You're lucky you found me - one uncaring woman.

You're not uncaring. Dylan said gently.

Nadia ran into hysteria. Nadia doubled over. Nadia was not made with feelings. Nadia came with a life time guarantee on feeling-immunity. She was a Strongwoman. A Strongwoman who took on One Word boys. And One Word Cement started forming small pools of liquid. Like they had forgotten their solid days.

So the Beetle and Nadia went for a late drive while Nishanthi listened to Hindi movie songs on the radio to stay up. She always waited for Nadia to come back home. The Short Term Word Syndrome dug out other things that Nadia thought were successfully banned. Like things that were known to be there in a relationship. They were to be called things for lack of clarity at this point. They were a little murky and hazy. They called for greater inspection of the Delusional Miss Nadia's Emotional Status, the existence of which had not been known up to then.

The blind of course fell in love. Just that it wasn't easy. And when the blind didn't fall in love with the blind, things were not easy - things become difficult and disquieting. And Nirmaleen would have laughed derisively if she knew Kala under-rated the difficulties. The blind fell in love with the voice, then the laughter. And then the touch. And then there would be the tormenting process of getting over the voice, then the laughter and the touch and the trickiest part was getting over words. Words that would haunt the mind until the blind felt down and upset about liking those who could see. Until the blind would curse the irritation of Blind Love. And people like Kala didn't see the blind that cried. Nirmaleen had the Stars to talk to. And the pillow that she called 'Pinkie' that now had a white pillowcase.

Rituals With Sumi-I

"I get the first mouth."

"That was the first mouth."
"No. What you're having now is the first mouth."
"That was the first mouth."
"Then, which is this one?" Sumi demanded. She always demanded Kala thought. Very bossy. Very ugly bossy. She hated bossy bosses. She liked benign bosses. Why couldn't Sumi be benign?
"Learn to count missy."
"You're cheating. I want the first mouth tomorrow."
"If you get the first mouth tomorrow that's definitely cheating."

Sumi couldn't reply. Because the third mouth of food was hers. The odd numbers were hers for the day. The meat entitlement was different of course. The mouth basis applied only for rice.

"Do you like the posters?" Kala mentally bit nails.
"Maybe a little," Dylan shrugged.
"Just a little, is it?" Kala carefully examined the posters that she did for the Church Cheap Fair, trying to be critical.
"Maybe." Dylan looked even cockier than usual, worse than even Superman.
"Why do you look as if ten hundred things are on your head?"
"Ten hundred - do you have to make numbers look weird as well?"
"Ten hundred is like thousand."
"Oh! OK."
"Well, what's going on in your head? Anything wron-gh?"
"Nothing's wron-ghhh."
He inflated his nostrils just like she did.
"Oh OK, felt a little obligated you know, since I'm your friend and stuff."

"Thank you for being my friend and stuff."
"How did your father die?"
Sudden, cruel, harsh tone.
Dylan ignored her. The air was filled with quiet, rusty, aged tones that carried heavy barrels of iron.
"Was it a rude question?"
"Maybe." He shrugged in a quiet, rusty aged sort of way, as if they carried heavy barrels of iron.
"You don't want to talk about it?"
"Maybe not."
The air reeked of rusty iron barrels. Smoky and hazy, battling for a little clarity in quietness. Almost with a twinge of agedness.
"OK."
"He died when I was six."
"OK."
"We used to make kites together."
"Really."
"I always lost them while flying."
Kala smiled.

Kala's diary: the second last page (where it was reserved for notes).
The mind requires emancipation at some point when it realizes that there is nothing solid or worthwhile about infatuation. There is nothing solid about conversations that are supposedly attractive and difficult to forget. The mind sends repeated appeals, almost nagging, since it realizes that emancipation must come fast for survival. How can a man take complete control of the thoughts - and all types of them? How can a man take control of the mind and all its demarcations. And Mind Citi-

zens would hold up placards clamoring for emancipation. Poor Mind Citizens – how they all look worried. Panicked almost.

How Emancipation is to be Obtained

Make resolutions – difficult ones to keep but those that would be effective enough to acquire emancipation. (Little notices that read 'Don't Be a Slave') They won't last long because the household will discover the notices and destroy them. But it's still worth it – given that emancipation is all that the mind requires to feel normal again. Destroy communication modes and instruments – like walks outside. Like mandatory church meetings. Like accidental bus meetings. Like voluntary poster sessions. Occupy the body – when the body becomes too occupied the mind has no time to feel anything apart from the grief generated by physical fatigue.

"Dylan you know the nicest stuff is the unexpected stuff." She laughed and blew away strands of hair that blurred the right eye.
"OK."
"Like things you think wouldn't happen but they happen – so you're happy."
"OK."
"You don't think so, do you?"
"No."
"Why?" She asked gently. Very gently, as if talking to a hungry little bread thief.
"Because."
Kala waited.

"Because you think so," Dylan started laughing then and stuck his tongue.

"That wasn't really funny."

"Sorry." He laughed all over again.

"You are a really funny boy."

"At least."

"At least what?"

"Nothing really."

"You behave like a three year old and I find it difficult to have a mature conversation with you!" She should have known that Dylan was ineligible for mature conversations.

"So, this stuff about the unexpected stuff being the nicest is a mature conversation?" Dylan said rather maturely.

"It could have been."

"You're just a hoity-toity woman."

"What the hell?"

"Yes, full of statements and annoying ones."

"I don't know about you, but I think unexpected stuff is the nicest stuff."

Kala the emotionalist.

Dylan the skeptic.

"What is this unexpected thing that happened which turned out to be nice?"

"Nothing happened. Why do you always turn my thoughts into a big argument?"

She waved her hands this way and that way. He stood still with calm composure.

"Kala we might have to get help for you."

"For?"

"You can't be serious! It's really spelled out I think."

"What? That I can't handle a psychopath?"

"See, poor comprehension skills."

He folded his arms and waited. Kala felt like she was fighting a lost battle. So she made herself busy with her nails and ignored Dylan completely for the rest of the evening.

5

WHAT MADE GOOD GIRLS THEN WERE WELL-BEHAVED YOUNG women ready for marriage. Girls lived within those boundaries because they understood that their whole life depended on good behaviour. There were strict morals buzzed around that were secretly meant to be deterrents. Moral statements like a girl could not afford to make a mistake or the more horrible ones like purity was all that mattered to a young woman. They had a huge impact even on those who outwardly shrugged off the morals. Because they knew better. No matter whether they shrugged it off or not - what the majority believed determined their marriageability. And all girls dreamt of a safe and secure marriage. To hell with liberal thoughts. Liberal thoughts of the few who thought the moral code was absurd, just managed vindication under the breath.

Dylan the Humanitarian as per findings of Kala

"Do you want me to buy toffees for you?"
"Toffees?"
He nodded.

"Why?" Kala asked almost alarmed.

"Just."

"What type?"

"All types. I want you to try out all types."

"Are you crazy?"

"You don't like toffees?" Dylan looked dismayed as if Kala had just told him that she did not love him.

Kala shook her head.

"Coffee?"

"Coffee." Kala nodded.

He ordered coffee.

"Would you ask for two?" she said awkwardly as if he were going to order only one.

"OK." After they sat down with the coffee Dylan looked up suddenly, "Will you taste mine?"

"It's the same thing." This was embarrassing she thought, like having coffee was not bad enough.

"It's not. This is another type." He pushed it across the table over to her. Kala Mind Elves stood by, some hung onto Kala's chair. The cheekier elves stood on Dylan's spiked hair. "It's different." Kala smiled. "Will you taste mine?"

"I've tasted it before."

"Tell me how it tastes then," Kala demanded.

He tried to remember, "I don't remember."

She pushed it across the table. "Could you use your straw?" she asked almost embarrassed.

Dylan agreed.

"It's nice." The Humanitarian smiled. And Mind Elves grunted and shook their heads.

When the SNAP rule came to be a lot of things changed. For example - perspective. Things that were looked at with giddy hope received quiet boredom. The SNAP rule had an important lesson to teach - SNAP caned until palms turned red and itchy. Till the intensely stupid knew they were intensely stupid. The intensely stupid began to look at the concept of forever more philosophically. That was a sad way to learn a lesson like that. Because SNAP had a bitter edge to it. Almost as if forever did not exist. So when SNAP returned afresh with Sumi's first death anniversary, Kala decided that infatuations were secondary to grief. People like Dylan had very little space in her heart.

Tree-House Making Technicalities: Bid to clear the way

"What are camera lenses that see far called?"

"You missed dinner Dylan."

"What are camera lenses that can see far?"

"Where were you during dinner?"

"You don't know, do you?" He should have known. Mother was a dumb woman who only lived to have a husband.

"Ask your father Dylan."

Father-II? Was she for real? This was the Ifthemovieweretobe! Mother didn't understand. This was his Tree House. It was his father, not hers. Mother's husband should not have anything to do with Thaththi's Tree House. The next day at the annual Cheap Fair Dylan broke into tears demanding that mother buy a picture that showed off a Tree-House. Dylan hung it in the room and looked at it between sums, between pictures, between moral lessons, between grammar. Between mornings and nights. Never mind the name for camera-like lenses that could see far. He would make a Tree House one day. Just like Thaththa would have - if only he were not-dead. Ifthemovieweretobe.

Rituals With Sumi –II

"If we had a pin we could have drawn smiley faces on wax drops."
"But that would be really - you know - kiddish," Sumi opined after careful thought. And chin scratching.
"I suppose," Kala sighed.
"Let's sing a song."
"OK," Kala giggled.
"Let's make up a song."
"Oh candles are burning. Do I have to write the words down - I don't have a note book." Kala, all worried that the best selling hit would be buried like a forgotten memory.
"It's OK. We'll do our proper songs later." Post-thought and chin-scratching.
"Hmmm."

> *Oh candles making patterns on the floor*
> *Candle light so pretty*
> *Kan---------duls are my love*
> *Car---------mmmmm to me my love (Very High)*
> *Kan-derls give me lie-fffff*
> *Kandles are my love (Ending low)*

And then they broke into breathless laughter. The candle fire played shapes on the walls and they watched till night till Sumi decided that her eyes hurt a little.

Saving feelings would have been the saddest thing that Nadia would have imagined. She tried to assess. There had to be a mistake somewhere. When she thought back to Dylan she had a bad feeling she had some saved feelings. So she decided that it was time to clean up old accounts. Now that she knew that there were old accounts saving feelings. The Castle of Perfection was to be Fully Restored. Just like it used to be. Feelings that snuck in without her permission must be publicly caned for what they were. The Castle of Perfection was nothing. Was it not? Careless hands and hips mocked it. Sniggered sarcastically. Downed vodka over it and laughed raucously. Like itdidntmatter. The Castle of Perfection was ruined in the sad discovery of feelings Nadia. Shut up! The Castle of Perfection is dead. Gone. Fuck off.

"Nadia sounds like a nice person."
"Nadia *is* a nice person."
"I meant it."
"I don't care whether you meant it or not, I think she's probably one of the smartest kids I've met with so much personality." And Jealousy woke up with a start with thin beads of perspiration on its nose.
"Well, I just wanted to make it clear that I was sincere."
"But nobody doubted it."
"Smartasss!" she chortled.
"Most conversations do not have a purpose Kala. They are all meant to fill the space of time. Unless of course you're some big-shot like Bill Clinton who always had so many smart things to say."

"You think he said smart things? Because that's a really smart thing to say," she chuckled.

"Smarter than you!"

"How if I fell in love? Do you think it will be difficult?"

"Are you in love?" He looked amused. As if she couldn't. She looked away.

"Me?"

"You?"

He waited.

"No."

"Sure?"

"Do I look confused?" she asked sarcastically.

He shrugged. "Do you think trees fall in love?"

"Maybe. It must be fun to be a tree and fall in love with another." She laughed away holding her stomach to balance herself.

He rolled his eyes.

"What now? What did I say?"

"You were speaking sense as usual."

She rolled her eyes back.

This was going to be a big day. Some fateful (or fateless for that matter) day. The stars shone a little less that night. As if aware that Nirmaleen would have other thoughts. Nirmaleen was to have more grown up thoughts. Thoughts about flutes and flute teachers. Amila came in and said hello in a very proper manner. The proper manner was defined by Nirmaleen's mother. Redefined again by Kala as a little puny. (In an undertone). Proper/puny had everything to do with how the hands clutched each other and the plain dress code and awkward smiles. So. Amila was a proper boy.

What was Dylan? Kala asked mother casually. Laughingly. As if a comparison would be oh-so-not-important. Mother asked back, with squinted eyes - the boy from church? Yes. Well he's proper I suppose. Kala brushed it aside as unimportant. Oh-So-Not-Important. Amila said he taught how flutes worked. Nirmaleen nodded and sat with her knees together. Nirmaleen smiled in all directions. Just like she always did. He smiled back, realizing it couldn't matter much. But Nirmaleen heard him smile. And waited till he smiled again. He used magical words, Nirmaleen thought. As if he had witnessed the mid-wife help words to come into the world. She felt him speak. It was difficult to explain, but she felt an unusual level of awareness when he spoke. Almost powerful. Goose bumps rose. Eyes felt wet. Moments were shorter - as if aware of their heightened level of importance. And as her flute lessons went on, it was difficult to ignore that he filled her mind. Shit! she thought. He was going to be a difficult flute teacher.

Three and half years later at the grand ceremony that had become custom in Sri Lankan society, Nirmaleen would wear a pink-gray sari. And she would refuse to dry clean it - claiming she never trusted the dry cleaners. She would wear lipstick for the first time in her life. She would thank God for blind eyes. For the first time. For the first time she would believe people who said the beautiful lashes stole the sight.

Rituals with Sumi-III

"Why did they invite us?"
"I didn't ask. That would have been like adding new meaning to it, wouldn't it?" Kala smiled from the corner of her mouth.
"You find it funny?"

"What do I find funny?"
"Being invited to a dumb party?"
"No. I think it's very offensive! Very offensive!"
"Why?" Sumi demanded.
"Everyone knows that we hate their parties. I think it's unspeakably offensive."
"Un-speakkkk-bly," Sumi echoed with considerable rage Kala thought. "What's this anyway?"
"It says: it's a party."
"Why?" Sumi demanded passionately.
"Are you saying that I encouraged the invitation?"
"No. Of course not. Only wondering."
"Don't."
Sumi ripped it making Fresh Paper Ripping Noises. Kala thought it was the right thing to do.

Amila was an odd boy. He was cute. With a moustache that had been disciplined rather crudely. With loose fitting t-shirts and pants that a man double his size could easily slip on. Amila practiced the flute with a passion. It was one part of his life where he felt he was in control. Those were important words for a boy-man of twenty. He didn't look at young women. Young women were defined as those who had long hair with a height exceeding four feet. That was the rudimentary quality of a Proper/Puny boy. Proper/Puny boys did not look at young women. He shoved off whenever romance or anything close crept in. So when he met Nirmaleen, he started shoving vigorously.

"Kala do you dance?"
"No."
"Dance with me."
"I don't dance."
"It's OK. Break a rule."
"I don't break rules."
"Do it for me."
"I don't like doing things for you Dylan."
"Why the hell are you here if you don't like parties?"
"Why are *you* here?"
"Hell, I have nothing against them."
"I used to hay-ttt parties." She shuddered.
"Because Sumi hated them?"
"Maybe."
"That's stupid."
"Are you calling Sumi stupid?"
"Not really. Maybe just you."
"Why don't you ask someone else to dance with you? I'm only here because I had to come."
"You won't dance with me?" Small light voice.
"No."
"Are you about to cry?"
"No."
"Did I say anything?"
"No."
"Kala, you can tell me."
"There's nothing to tell."
"People cry when they are sad."
"People cry for joy too," Kala muttered.
"Oh, so this is one of those?"

"Yes."

"You look nice tonight." Small light voice.

"OK."

"I think 'Thank you' is the word."

"I don't care."

"Tell me why you look sad."

"I'm not sad."

"People are going to think we have something going on, the way we are now." They were in a dark corner of the party hall, where dim lights made dark corners look even dimmer.

"What people think doesn't matter."

"Yes."

"You look very nice tonight Kala."

"You told me that once."

"I said you are nice, not very nice."

"OK."

"Kala I feel a little sloshed."

"That's nice. Even I feel a little high."

"Why are you upset? I won't remember it tomorrow since I'm sloshed."

"Why would I pour my heart out to a drunk man?"

"Because I'm nothing to you." Small light voice.

Poor Kala. Poor Kala. Poor Kala and Bushes and Mud Pools. Poor Kala and Bushes and Mud Pools and the Night Air. Kala and Company. Kala and Company registered under Depression Laws. Elegant company for a sad mind. No eloquent words. Bushes wilted. Mud pools burped. Here. There. Night Air watched. And hummed a little. Not too much. Kala liked Dylan?

No. Kala liked Dylan! NO! KALA LIKED DYLAN! FUCK OFF!

Sumi would have called her mad. Sumi would have said the old Kala had disappeared. Sumi would have hugged her long enough to make sure things were not this awful. Sumi would have asked Dylan to go to hell. Go to hell. Go to hell you bastard! Yep, she would have asked him to stay the hell away. He couldn't have held against Sumi. Sumi would have found another guy for her. Sumi would have made sure Dylan felt like a complete loser when she danced with the other guy. Sumi would have made sure that Dylan could never forget that he was a complete jerk who deserved nothing.

"Go out with me."
"Why?"
"I like you."
"I can't."
"Go out with me."
"This is not funny."
"I like you."
"You don't love me." She looked down and waited. Waiting for denial. Waiting for a passionate rejection. Even angry.
"Go out with me." He asked softer this time.
"I should go home."
"Can I walk you home?"
"Why?"
"Just."
"There are angels protecting those who walk in the night."
"What are they like?"
"Haven't seen them." She shook her head.

"Do you believe they are around?"
"Yes."
"Go out with me."
"Don't play with friendships - it's a sin."
"I'll ask for forgiveness later."
"Have to go home."
"Good Night!" Rusty. Buried. Noisy.
"You too."
Footsteps getting lighter. Footsteps were harder to get. Footsteps gone. Footsteps difficult access channel to mind. Footsteps didn't tell a sad story. Footsteps were nothing. Footsteps only walked. Dylan went back inside.

Kala's diary: June 3rd

I'm the weakest woman I know. I can't breathe in peace. It's not fair that an obsession is one way. I feel pathetic. I'm the weakest. A speck and a leaf. A mild cough and tuberculosis. A surge and a stroke. A wave and a Tsunami. I'm a fragmented mind with no strong thoughts. I need a man who speaks the same passion. Not a boy who fancies me. I am the weakest for not killing this beast. I sit for dinner and smile. I ask Nirmaleen how her day has been. I eat bread in silence. I wait for you in my mind. My fragmented mind makes up hasty dreams of you to make me happy. I'm a smile and well of tears. There's no balance in me. I'm hopelessly obsessed. I remember a word you mentioned. I dream intensely. I wonder about you constantly. I grow weaker. I'm drowned. This wonderful drowning sensation. This hellish wonder.

"Will you stay for tea Amila?" Nirmaleen asked very shyly. She was careful, slow and very careful not to stutter.

"Yeh." It came too quickly. There was no "s". He swallowed it, as if he only realized half way that he said yes. So it was too late. Tea was such a weird drink. Just a cup of tea incorporates chatter. Glances at the watch with mixed emotions. Giddy laughter. One sided furtive looks. She flapped lashes and laughed. He watched her flap lashes. He always watched. But they were all performed for a cup of tea. Even for the Proper/Puny it seemed a tad farcical.

"I love how it feels in my hand," he said, as they began a flute conversation.

She flapped lashes. Smiled. Flap-smiled.

"You feel as if you are in control?"

"Yes," she said surprised that he captured it so well. Nirmaleen wiped her palm against the skirt of the frock that showed off a vague pattern of wild flowers on white. She flapped lashes.

"What do you do when you don't study Amila?"

"What do you do?"

She smiled. He touched her finger and then drew it back before she could register the touch properly.

"I love the sound it creates." It came out suddenly.

"I do too," he said. But didn't add anything.

"It sounds like an interlude to some place greater, doesn't it?" she asked.

"Yes. Is that why you like it?"

"Yes. It makes me see," she whispered. "You know?"

"I know."

"I wish I could see your face." She flapped lashes. He said nothing. She laughed, embarrassed.

"It's much easier for you then," he muttered under his breath.

Tea was over. He got up and walked out. She heard the gate unlatch and latch back.

Kala snapped the switch off and decided to play a candle game that night. The type she used to play when she was nine. There was something strangely consoling about practicing childhood rituals. They made Kala feel that nothing beyond nine was real. Things beyond nine didn't matter. The only person who mattered in the post-nine era was dead. Candle games required three lit candles erected in a triangle. Then the favorite songs were sung - in the softest of the voices. There should be no sound to the outside world. That was considered sacrilegious. But the mobile started beeping. And beeping. And beeping. How amusing caller ID seemed then. Curiosity nipped in the bud. Like a press release lacking sensation. But there were other emotions that filled in for curiosity - for example the mad urge to click the 'Answer' button and crack hello. But past incidents called for discipline. Rigorous discipline. And so the call was missed.

But then it started beeping again. And continued to beep. Suddenly the phone was not an inanimate object anymore. It carried a distinct pleading expression and then a mocking expression, as if aware of the torment caused. Pleading and snorting. Snorting and pleading. Pleading and snorting. Really pushing it Kala thought, because she would dash it on the floor any moment. Or worse yet, answer. But who could go through the post-call ordeal? Besides who knew what the conversation was to contain? So the call was missed again. What created such complexity in the mind and caused a bloody battleground? Torment had a way of shattering the mind's sanity and reveling in absurdity. Phones pleaded and snorted. Minds blew noses grossly and sighed heavily.

Kala sang away, until the head stopped. The heart stopped. The mind started clapping in a giddy state as if this were some consolatory form of entertainment. And then it stopped embarrassed, realizing that this was no conclusive end to torment. This was bitter exhaustion. This would start all over and grieve again.

Rituals were also practiced on the other side. He tore paper to tiny shreds. Tinier shreds. Until they grew smaller and smaller. And mother showed up at the doorway half-bemused by the activity. Aware that mother was there, he resisted the temptation to look up. Why should he? Angry people did not lift their head. Angry people hated lifting heads to clash eyes. Eye-clashing didn't happen for the angry. Angry people only loved paper and shredding it to tiny bits.
"Is it OK?" She asked glancing at him and back at the empty chair next to him.
He shook his head.
But she sat.
Why bother to ask? Probably a pretext to make conversation. The nerve!
"You want a hand?"
He looked up - time for eye-clashing - real bloody eye-clashing. But she took a tiny piece and started slashing it to smaller shreds. He eyed her hands and ignored her.
"What's up Dylan? You look very down."
No kidding.
She touched his hand and tried again. "Do you want to talk about it?"
GET OUT mother. This really isn't the time to brush up on maternal touch.
Too bad mother couldn't read thoughts. Too bad mother was encouraged by silence.

"You know that you can always talk to me. Right Dylan?"
Right.
Breeze crept through and the shreds of paper started partying on the table. So he crushed the partying with his fingertips. Mother left the room. She was an unwanted extra, it was too embarrassing to be around when the role was an extra and unwanted.

6

Kala's diary: one of the "notes" pages.

I was in a room - a cell like room. There were windows that were like holes with ugly bars. There was nothing pretty about the room. Just a plain room. With me inside. But was that me? There was a girl in a pale white dress, ruffled hair, average shaped legs that were only half shaven. She groped about. Unfamiliar with the cell. But there was no oppression. No fear. No impatience. Just curiosity to understand. There was a light inside the cell - almost heavenly. A beautiful ray of light that filtered in from above, from one of the barred holes. But the girl groped about. Curiosity? But maybe that's a misperception. Maybe she was trapped. And looked for a way out.

Immediate Events after the Short Term Word Syndrome

There was nothing solid about feelings. They just introduced unnecessary trouble to the mind. She bought a Smirnoff on the way and went upstairs. One big bottle with one big girl. No knocks were entertained. No dinner downstairs, in bed with a headache.

Could Nishanthi come in please just to check the temperature please? No. Thank you. She can manage without anyone. Could Nishanthi bring some warm water? Please? Nadia Baba sounded very sick indeed. Nishanthi go away. Don't bother me.

Nishanthi go away. Don't bother me. Nishanthi had no clue what feelings could do to a woman allergic to them. She could very well die. How could bloody warm water help? This was emotional calamity. There was no tangible cure. She was very drunk by the time mother knocked on the door.
"I heard you're sick."
"Yes. But I'm not."
"What's wrong?"
"Nothing."
"Warm water?"
"Good night mother!"
"Good night darling!"
Relief in the voice. How loving mother was. She asked how she was and offered warm water. Good night mother. Can I go really? Can I? Have your warm water bath mother. Daughter just drinking away mother. Emotionally pawned. Emotional leper! They thought she was a fool who knew nothing about stuff like feelings. Oh, but she had them too. She had come to know them. One more down the throat! One more to kill feelings.

This was a world of Conversationalists who were ready to help the Delusional. They stood in unusually erect positions. Clad in white. Humming tunes of Compassion. They made a quirky noise that made normal people want to block their ears. It wasn't unpleasant. Not hip. Not upbeat. Just a noise supposedly sedative. Nadia let out a loud cackle. She swung her skirt this way and that. Paced slowly. Felt the cold grass beneath. The place was beautiful. Nadia swung her head this way and that. The air smelled of flowers. Like a flower garden. There were so many. Nadia smiled. Breathed blissfully. Conversationalists smiled and whispered hello and ignored the hand Nadia held out to grasp. As if she was an untouchable. The grass blended with soft sand that played between her toes. Maybe they didn't know who she was.

"Will you miss me if I go away?" Kala asked.
"Where will you go?"
"If I go away?"
"You won't go."
"If I go away?"
"Where?"
"Miss me then?"
"No!" He started laughing. "Did you watch a loser movie?"
"No."
"Well, you sound as if you have." The laughter continued. Loud and permanent.
"You won't miss me?"
"No!" Dylan laughed. Kala watched.

Kala watched the rain - wanting to distract herself. The rain had a lovely pattern, like drunken dancers at a pub. The raindrop clatter filled the ears and they moved so fast that they blinded the eyes as well. But they helped because they distracted the mind, which now sent desperate appeals for emancipation. How sweet then did Estrangement sound! Estrangement never challenged the mind. It dried the mind. That was all. And the rain kept trying its best to distract the mind until it was exhausted with its charms.

Day Three since surprise disclosure of the Short Term Word Syndrome

Bottle on the floor. Tissues on the table. Unused of course. Nadia didn't cry. Unless at a school play ages back. Bottle on the bookrack. Unfinished as yet. Tequila. Not strong enough. Bloody mild tequila. How bloody. Pencils on the bed, with paper of course. Letters to Self. That only made sense on an abstract level. She got bored writing them really. Boredom was a hollow. That probably meant that she had no other feelings. But then in the morning – there would be a fresh onslaught by Feelings. And Nadia would feel Feelings. A whole lot of them.

Conversationalists walked by without much conversation. Nadia sat down and joined in the quirky murmur. It was unfeeling murmur, uninterpretable. She had declared loud enough for everyone that she was, well, she was Nadia. Some had continued to murmur as if they could not hear. Some had stooped their heads and grinned (not particularly at her) and continued to murmur. Then there was an inscription on a wooden plank: DELUSIONAL APPOINTMENTS - CONVERSATIONALIST V
Hello Nadia
Hello?
You may call me Conversationalist V
Nadia arched her brows and laughed lightly, the way she did when she felt superior. Conversationalist V wore large gypsies in his earlobes.
What happened to you Nadia? Conversationalist V stared back as if something had actually happened to her.
What happened to me?
What happened to you Nadia? He was soft. And slow. Like he knew. Like he knew what happened. And this was just to rack her mind. To

make her cry.
What. Happened. To. Me.
Nothing Nadia. You're Perfect.
And then he broke into loud, (scathing, Nadia thought) laughter.

The boss was a lighthearted man who cared for his subordinates. The boss leered and made pathetic comments which fuelled lunch-time humour. They discussed how boss was the most incompetent man they knew. They didn't know that good looks were part of the game and made up for lack of competence. Boss bought ice-cream for his team on Fridays before they left. They ordered all types of flavours and the office boy made a pretty sum on the variety rich ice cream bag. They lost count of which cost what. Besides the boss didn't like looking cost conscious for fifty rupees or so. It wasn't important.

The boss was a caring man. He noticed when his all girl team looked stressed out and asked them to go home early if they didn't feel up to it. The bank made easy profits on booming investment prospects. Giving them a day off to relieve stress was easy enough for a divisional manager like boss.

The boss was a good looking man who dressed to kill on most days. He had a collection of Le Bond shirts that made his big build look educated. His face looked competent. Kala thought he could have been good looking if he didn't leer the way boys practiced at fourteen. She always nodded professionally at meetings with him, even when she knew he came up with non-commendable ideas that could fuel lunch room humor. That was the best way to humour his Le Bond-ed face.

Dylan sat down. Dylan hated bitches. Dylan hated food without salt. Kites were pretty only if they could fly. Broken kites presented problems to boys who spent hours making them. Bloody sad then. When boys asked girls out they say: yes. I didn't hear that! A little louder now! Yes please! And the boy would kiss obligingly. And then the love story began. And then bitches tore into ruined age-old theories. What did bitches say? Bitches shook their heads and walked away as if unaware of the humiliation caused. Kites that couldn't fly. Bitches that couldn't utter yes! Dylan threw away the food. Tasteless bloody thing. Spineless tart.

Day Five since the surprise discovery mentioned earlier

Nishanthi thought Nadia should see the Doctor. It had been long enough, hadn't it? It had indeed. So what? Die over it? She had tried medication. What medication? Not like Nadia Baba to get medication that early anyway. Stop lying Nadia Baba. Nishanthi, if you bother me, I will tell them you are a bother. They will send you away.
"Open the door Nadia!"
"Why?"
"Why not?"
"Go away. I'm sick."
"Can I come in for a bit sweetie?"
"No!"
"Do you have fever?"
Trick One. The Go Away Trick. Gentle tone: "I'm better now. Please, I like to be alone. For a bit at least."
Footsteps fading.
Tucker-Tuk Tuk.

Tuk.
Tuk.
Tuk.
Ter.
Gone.
Good, she thought. Always worked with Daddy. Guru of filial awareness. How dark the night was. Dreary dark.

Dear Dreary Dark,

I think you are the sexiest thing that the earth has. Imagine, you can hold things that nobody could see. Incidentally, I thought I would mention I have come to sense the presence of Feelings. No matter of course. They are to disappear soon. I know, a real hogwash, are they not? They hurt too. As if I asked them over!
Sincerely,
Nadia.

Wasn't sincerely like a Feeling? Not too wise to use that expression, was it? She would sound hypocritical - not a very good first impression. As if I asked them over (tragic bunch are they not?) Nadia. Where did the bottle go? The bed - under it. Empty bottles reposing under the bed.

Guess!
I wouldn't know.
Come on!
I really wouldn't. Nadia struggled to break free. But he was too strong for her. He had his hands wrapped over her eyes.
Come on!!!
I wouldn't know you jobless freak!
My name is Conversationalist C.

Like CC? Nadia asked.

Like City Council! He had very hairy hands that made them look almost black.

He grinned absurdly.

Nadia shuddered back.

What happened to the Castle of Perfection Nadia?

Nothing.

We heard about it here Nadia.

So?

We know that you suffered a mammoth loss.

What loss? It didntmatter anyway!

Those are tunes of compassion you hear Nadia. They hear pain all the time. Pain like yours. We heard about it here Nadia.

What do you know? She whispered.

We know you lost everything.

Conversationalist C leaned forward to touch her face. But she ran. Confounding the sand in the grass.

"Can you hold it properly now?"

"Yes it feels like a part of me. That's how it should be right?"

"Yes," Amila sounded almost twenty-six. Like he grew up at flute lessons.

"What do you do in school?"

"I play the flute." Simple and direct answer with no incentive to chat, if that was what she wanted. Best that way. He waited, almost afraid that he offended her. She shook her head seriously, as if there had been some deep misunderstanding. "I mean like studies. What do you do?"

"Science." Simple and direct.

Nirmaleen didn't think he was simple and direct at all. She thought he was actually obliging. May be a little formal, maybe. That she thought was probably because he was such a Proper boy.

"Even I want to do science!" Nirmaleen burst out gleefully. This new discovery was great. The Discovery of Common Interest. Even if she never disclosed Common Feelings, this seemed like a satisfying compensation. He didn't say anything. And then he asked whether she would like to participate in a special concert for flutists.

"Me? Noooooo."

She flapped lashes. He watched. Flap. Flap. He looked away.

"You can, if anyone can," he said softly.

"You don't think they will laugh at me?"

"Nobody will."

Kala's diary: one of the "notes" pages.

This girl in the cell won't go away. As if this trap business were real. There are rusty little corners in the cell that look almost as though they were openings. But they aren't. Bloody delusion pits. Crude teasers. Am I supposed to be concerned by recurrent dreams? This girl looks scared now. I see fear and panic in the eyes now. But I'm hyper. Oh, the ray of light is gone. It's dark, except for delusion pits. She weeps (not too obviously). I interpret sounds that are akin to sobs. I feel sorry for her. Poor kid. This one's got the same tangled matted hair. So it's the same girl. This "court jester" in my head says it's me. But you know how court jesters are. Very cheeky. She's given up looking for a way out I think. I hope court jesters were beheaded for cracking unbecoming jokes.

"You've been lagging behind a bit, you know. Is there something bothering you?"

She shook her head.

"Are you sure? Because we can talk about it, even if it's not related to work."

When was this man going to get the drift? Why the hell would she talk to him about her 'not-related-to-work-problems?' "Kala, you're way behind your potential. Do you realize that?"

Women-user. Women-creepy-user. Women-poacher. Creepy poacher. Why couldn't he leave her alone? He adjusted his Le Bond-ed collar and sipped the tea the office boy had left carefully on one side of the table away from the computer.

Kala's diary: August 22nd

I wish there was rain tonight. Pretty rain that wakes up goose bumps. And the trees are lovely too I suppose. Kind of makes me wonder what I like in a man then. The trees are very pretty – who knows maybe they have conversations – gosh I'm beginning to sound like Nirmaleen! But the trees sway in a funny way that it's impossible not to think that they are not conferencing. They probably talk about reproduction! They can't not. I mean we are so obsessed with sex and stuff how can trees not be? But I hope they are not! It's nicer not to be.

Kala's diary: August 23rd

I guess all of us go through obsessions. We are all so bloody capable of them. They infect the mind and then infect the breathing patterns as well. I suppose they would be fun if they didn't hurt, if they didn't drench the mind and didn't cause awfully long and difficult colds - they would have been tolerable. But they are so difficult. The mother becomes obsessed with her child. That's OK though. Her love is unconditional; she expects nothing for her bout of obsession. So I suppose it doesn't hurt. But when there is no reciprocity when it's the very thing needed for the obsession to be gratifying it becomes difficult to sound as if the throat is fine. And worse yet, had been fine. The runny nose would make it very difficult, especially the sniffs. How strange it would be if anyone read all this crap! What would Dylan think of me? He'll probably think I've madly fallen for him! But obsessions are sad - because I'm not a mother - and I certainly don't love a child.

Dylan the Humanitarian as per findings of Kala

Sad little Kala Mind Elves walked by trying to make Kala understand that love wasn't a hateful feeling. Some murmured how rude Kala was. They were told off. She waited for the humanitarian to come and make her feel better. Elves weren't self-centered. So they hoped the humanitarian would come. Kala looked at the watch. Elves looked at the watch. Some Elves thought she needed help. Hel-ppp. But they kept their thoughts to themselves.
"Hello."
"What are you doing here?" Kala sounded surprised.
"Why? Can't I be here?"
Smile. Humanitarian smile that made the unfortunate feel fortunate. Kala smiled. The Elves watched.
"Are you OK?"
"Yes." Kala smiled again. Elves stared back.

Kala's diary: August 24th

I had a funny dream today - I imagined you performing ballet on the tip of my nose - like I said kind of funny but it was very pleasant too. How strange dreams are? I could really laugh - you as a ballet dancer doesn't add up. Well, I really hope this long tiresome obsession for you would end - I wonder how far dementia is?

The flute had become a tired subject. The flute teacher was tired. The flute student was tired-er. Amila's dilemma was not a moral one. It was more a big bloating fact that stood heavy with drooping earrings and a large stomach earned by an excessive intake of cholesterol and virtually no exercise. He feared what she might say about a blind girl. He almost knew his mother would find it unacceptable. Much later, his wife's assertion that he was being a typically liberal father would be woefully wrong. Amila learned lessons at twenty (while imparting lessons on the flute) to be a Father and a Mother. To be a proper son. To be a responsible flute teacher and as a result a very tired one. Proper/Puny (or Puny/Proper) boys hated displeasing their mothers. She almost sensed the restraint. She felt it. Even through the tenderness it came stomping, with thick boots on. She knew about things like restraint. Even through blissful flute tunes came the sounds of restraint like a drain of waste water. So there was chatter over tea on Subjects of Importance. Subjects of Importance were defined as those that had a direct academic bearing. Flute lessons were embraced on a platonic tone always - he liked being called Aiya (elder brother). She liked being called Nangi (younger sister) on the same basis.

"You have to concentrate, remember they only want to listen to you." He watched her hands while talking to her. Fingers danced. Trembled. Stopped. Trembled. Stopped again. Scared. Embarrassed. Trembled. She had beautiful hands and nails cut short - they looked clean and rosy - almost like a child's. The flute made it difficult not to touch her. He tried to concentrate on the wooden strip. The wooden strip plaited between rosy fingers. Rosy fingers with a wooden strip between. Rosy fingers. Rosy fingers with clipped nails.

"Imagine the tune in your head. It helps."

She flapped lashes. Smiled. He smiled. Flap-watched.

"You better wear something nice."

"Are you teasing me?"

"No, I am not."

She heard him smile. She punched him in the stomach calling him a rat!

"Rats are quite nice actually!"

"Funny, coz I've been told they are ugly and miserly!"

"But now you know differently!" Amila laughed. And watched. Trembled still. Stopped. Embarrassed. Nirmaleen laughed.

Rituals with Sumi-IV

"Bring some more water."

"But we might get caught!"

"So? Are you afraid?"

"No!" Kala got the water. Shivered as the water made noise as it landed on the pail. Very ugly bossy. She should rebel for benevolence.

Sumi and Kala Environmental Foundation in action.

"Who will water if we don't at this time?"

"Nobody." Sumi was right. School plants would dry and die if they didn't water when they stayed to camp out at school.

"But it makes so much noise," Kala protested. "If we get caught?"

Unanswered. Ignored as if Kala thoughts were unimportant. As if Kala thoughts made no sense. Kala looked away.

There were huge bubbles of hurt all around. They burst one by one with a tiny pop sound that echoed slightly. Kala crushed some of them but they were not solid enough for the grasp of the hand. She kept telling herself that it was a dream - there were no bubbles in real life - but then an older woman came up to her and told her not to crush the bubbles. She muttered sorry and looked down because she noticed that there were others too and they did not harm the bubbles.

So maybe this was real after all. Maybe Bubbles of Hurt did exist. She searched for a familiar face for reassurance. But they were very unfamiliar. And the bubbles continued to parade and she watched and knew that in truth the hand must destroy them and not allow them to die naturally. But then the woman would come over and make a racket and that would be embarrassing. Better let them die quietly. But how she would have loved crushing them!

On the way home in public transport Kala flirted. Flirting was tricky and tren dy. Flirting with those unknown was trendier.

(1) The potential garment factory machine operator

He had a tiny moustache and wore tweed trousers with a size 16-collar shirt. Kala thought he had white teeth. She ignored the possibility of cavities. Or cavity fillings. He looked very tired but eager to flirt. She appreciated that. He must be from a garment factory, Kala surmised. She looked up twice. Good. He always returned the look-ups. What a pretty boy he was!

(2) The Marketing Executive

The Marketing Executive referred to as ME henceforth, carried a folded tie in his pocket. The woes of the profession. Tie, morning and day in tropical weather and rolled up to go home. ME had a pointed nose with tons of blackheads. Weather brown but very beautiful according to Flirt Kala. Kala smiled and offered to keep ME's files since ME was standing to make it easier for ME to grip inside a bus that drove wild. That helped to flirt too.

(3) The corporate executive in the car abreast

Flirt Kala tossed hair. Tucked hair behind ear. And then un tucked it. Pursed and unpursed lips just to make sure that they didn't look pale. She smiled and smiled back. She really couldn't see the face - hence no description. His social status derived from the car, the hands free mobile, a laptop case and some files in the back seat.

How sad flirting was. Because on the way she remembered Dylan. She smiled with him in her mind. How painful to miss him! *Kili herself?* What a sad ball game this whole shit bag of love was. How bloody uncontrollable. *Kill herself.* Life was a gift wrapped in lovely gold paper topped off with a shinier gold ribbon. She was going to be so happy one day. Happy with large cliché-toothpaste smiles. Smiles of various types spurred on by happiness. She'll have a husband and kids and all this will be forgotten. *Kill, kill, kill!* She shouldn't kill herself. Life was a gift. What a beautiful gifty!

Day Thirty-One since the discovery of Feelings of vulnerability et al

Write down Feelings that prowled.
Depression.
Hurt.
Vulnerability.
Wanting to be different.
Wanting to stand out.
Wanting to be loved. No. It couldn't be that. It had to be something else. But honesty is important Nadia if you want to find a cure. Proper diagnosis was crucial, she told herself.
Wanting to be loved. All right.
Wanting to be good (I think).

Dear good people,
    I realize I'm a bad girl. Always been one too. I never wanted to be a good girl. So try not to drag me into this moral shit hole. You the good fuckers are not even trying. I wish you did. I'm begging you now. Because you see this sort of radical shift (if it were to happen at all) would be difficult. Let me remind you that a bad girl among good people wouldn't be to your credit either.
Sincerely (she was addressing good people after all)
Nadia.

Does daddy love you Nadia?

Of course.

How much Nadia?

However much I would ask.

That's nice. Conversationalist D sniggered. Or maybe Nadia imagined.

But why then all these complaints? He sniggered again.

WHAT complaints?

Depression, hurt, vulnerability?

You eavesdropper! You metaphysical cheat!

Everybody knows about your emotional status and - he cleared his throat awkwardly and the quirky murmur got a little louder - what happened to the Castle of Perfection?

Daddy loves me!

Of course. There can be no mistake. Conversationalist D sniggered again as if on cue.

And the Castle of Perfection WILL be restored. And I don't need your pity.

You don't? Nadia you will die without my pity at this point. He sniggered quietly.

Daddy loves me!

And if he doesn't? What then?

But he does!

Does he know about your emotional status Nadia?

No. She looked down, humiliated by the blatantly ugly question.

Do you love daddy back?

Why?

Do you?

No. She whispered. Scary whisper. Whisper lost in fear.

"Nadia Baba breakfast."

"Bring it in."

"Madam and sir asked how you are Nadia Baba."

"Healthy. Thank you."

"No fever Nadia Baba!" Nishanthi cried delighted.

"Yes. I noticed."

"Nadia Baba don't drink when you're sick Nadia Baba. It's bad."

"Shut up and get out before I get very sick Nishanthi." Why was she so bloody concerned? She wasn't even related. She called the cat to the window and started feeding it toast.

Kala's diary: August 31st
(At Work)

> *Today I sat by the window listening to a rather long discussion. The AC chilled me. They didn't notice. Fools - obsessed by these bloody business variables. I nodded. Here. There. Comprehendingly. It got very cold then, unbearably. And I pictured you next to me. Holding my hand, to keep me warm. I could listen then, and nod, and comprehend. It made sense, this ring business. You see, I started circling this rather charming ring on my finger. I tried to think it was a gift from you. If it had been from you - it would have been so much easier to imagine you next to me. Holding my hand. We could listen, nod and comprehend. A radical thought of course. Imagine - Dylan, could I have a ring please? I need it when I am in the a/c without you! Probably why lovers wear rings. You touch fingers always. You feel them continuously. Imagine, I could touch you in my mind, and nobody sees. Lovers are smart aren't they? As dumb as they sound.*

The Historic Revelation of the Word: Re the Tree-House Movie

Mother looking through dictionary. Mother flips. Dylan waits. Dylan waits patiently. Dylan waits sanguinely. Dylan such a sanguine boy. Dylan needs to learn new words for exams to come. As per requirements of certain crucial subjects.

"Could you spell that for me?"

"She has it?"

"Shhhhh!!!!!"

"She has it?" Undertone.

Mother glared.

"Could you spell that for me Edith? **B-I-N-O-C-U-L-A-R-S** Thank you Edith wait, my son is here."

"Say thank you Aunty Edith." Undertone.

"Thank you Aunty Edith."

Women-user. Women-creepy-user. Women-poacher. Creepy-poacher. Why couldn't he leave her alone? Go away boss. I don't like it. I don't like it! But he was a benign boss who listened. What a benign boss. He reached and touched. Touched here. Touched there. And then she forgot to log his touches. They ran all over as if there were no restrictions. They ran incoherently as if it were everything ever anticipated. Benign boss being benevolent to Kala. Kala should be grateful, not every boss was this thoughtful. He knew she was depressed. She knew that he knew. How good knowing touches felt. Don't go away boss. Don't go away. And then he asked whether she was OK. Was she OK? She nodded. Better? Surely.

Kala's diary: September 4th

My mind is a mess of misery. How can one man replace another? Like a new toothbrush. Or a new plastic cup. I had my first kiss from my boss. Boss kissed me with passion. How can parody be real? I felt as if I was getting my compulsory vaccination for Rubella. Look what I've become. An unkissed kisser. Is there a cure for incessant delirium? I imagine a chained prisoner when I think of myself. I kissed flesh today. Felt spit in my mouth and when I think of a kiss my mind spotlights Dylan. So. I kissed without you.

The boss was a man who appreciated the pretty. He looked at Kala with enormous admiration. The type that grew in blubbers and flab. He was open in his praise. Boss liked making pretty comments about the pretty. It gave him a certain sense of satisfaction about his very palpable male flamboyance.

"You are very pretty."

"I am."

"I meant it."

"So did I."

"Will you be late to go home?"

"No. I don't like home."

"Why?"

"There's no one at home."

He touched the chin. How nice! He felt sorry. He felt so sorry. He ran his fingers full of sorry. Kala no home? Pretty Kala no home? How lugubrious. Dire-lugubria. Lugubrious bubbles. Big Lugubria Land full of bubbles. Huge bubbles to kiss away for boss. Boss to the rescue. Boss drag me out of bubble Lugubria. Boss conquers Lugubria Land. Boss I love you! Boss I love your art of bubble land cure. Sorry Fingers such fun boss!

Rituals with Sumi-V

"But I like this better."
"It's horrible."
"See, it feels good too. See it's easy to walk in them. See, they are not too high either. See!"
"They look horrible."
Sumi thoughts on shopping were superior to Kala thoughts on shopping. Kala thoughts were horrible. Kala thoughts made no sense. Kala thoughts were unimportant.
"See. They look much nicer. Better than that horrible pair."
"OK. Then it's this."
"Ha! I knew you'd listen to me!"
Kala listened. Kala born with ears. Sumi made sense.
Sumi the decision maker. Kala the commoner with no common sense.

"You are late. Where were you? Do you know we were worried?" Mother demanded with one hand on the head and one on the hip.
"I'm sorry."
Didn't Kala look weird? Kala looked tired and disheveled. Kala looked as if things have changed.
"How did you come?"
"My boss dropped me home." *My boss played with me.*
"Why didn't you come early? Why did you come with boss?"

"Because I had work at office that I couldn't leave behind." *Because boss had so much to teach.*

Kala wasn't herself, mother thought. But she forgot about it when she remembered the kettle on the cooker. How careless of her! How much gas wasted. And gas prices were so high too!

"Would you have dinner with me Kala?"
"OK." *More sorry fingers boss? Why wouldn't I?* While in the car with him, her palms refused to cease gathering sweat between them. She casually swept them on the car seat to dry her palms. She spoke fast and almost incoherently. He asked then, "Are you alright? You seem a bit jumpy."

She looked at him and shook her head and started playing with the car stereo. She was a bit jumpy she supposed. But what the hell could she do, and more to the point what could he do?
"Are you alright Kala, you know that I won't hurt you. Don't you?" Kala's Humour Elves started doubling over then and kicked their feet in the air and took turns amongst themselves to peep through the curtains to catch a better glimpse of Nalaka looking gentlemanly. "Don't I?" She winked then.

He pulled back onto the road and started relating a childhood prank. She listened to the bit where he said he was seven and about as dumb as any seven year old was. What happened then? She lost focus. She wondered whether Dylan had a prankful childhood. He lost his dad early, so he probably didn't. He probably had an awful childhood with step dad pleased to cane him. Poor Dylan. What was the man next to her saying? Was he saying he lied to his mother about the bruises? That was pretty good, she thought. She hardly spoke to her mother. Let alone lie.

"You love your mother?"
"Of course I do! I just lied to get away. Any kid does that!"
"I just asked whether you love her."
"I do."

She looked out the window then and wondered what Sumi was doing then. Singing probably. She probably had a better voice now. Maybe she was an angel now. Sumi used to love singing. They always used to hum in class between lessons.
"If the bank does well this year the share prices are going to shoot up."
How did they get there? She must have asked something about the bank, and he probably couldn't help blabbering away.

"I hope I won't be alone one day," Nirmaleen whispers quietly.
"You won't," Kala whispers back.
"I will be, but I hope you won't be at least."
"I hope you will be happy Nee."
"I am." Nirmaleen smiles. Smiles completely. Till her lashes smile.
"You won't be alone. I will be there."
"Where?" Nirmaleen laughs.
"Here." Kala wraps Nirmaleen's hand in hers and places it on her chest.
"What are you upset about?"
"I'm OK. I always have been."
"You're not. I know that."
"Why do you think that?" Kala whispers.
"Because I'm your best friend."
My best friend was killed by a bloody lorry several years back. My best friend's death was the beginning of a fanatic infatuation.

"You are my sister." With a containment of mourn. With a sip of grief. Dab of tenderness.

"Are you sad?"

"No Nirmaleen."

"Don't be sad. Nothing's worth staying sad. And I love you."

"I love you too. Sadness makes you stronger sometimes."

"It makes you a complete ruin at other times."

"I'm OK. I will be."

"I don't want you to be sad. I'll be sadder than you are then. I know when you are sad. I feel it. I know your voice. I see more than you think."

7

KALA'S DIARY: SEPTEMBER 10TH

I think I've lost my virginity. But I didn't bleed. I'm not sure what he did. I know he used his fingers to do bloody something. But I can't ask anyone. Can I? I couldn't do anything. It didn't even occur to me that I should have said no. I could have done something. Oh well, it's gone if it's gone. I should have gone out with my elocution class friend. I should have found out what it was like to have a boyfriend at fourteen. It's too late for boyfriends. It's too late for innocent romance. There's only room for an unholy, repulsive affair. I let him touch me. I let him touch me. I let him touch me.

Then she drew tiny flowers at the edges of the diary and fell asleep. She saw pretty dreams that night. She was in a room that looked like a classroom. There were wooden desks and chairs, the type usually seen in classrooms. There were vaguely familiar faces. Her school friends. Even Sumi. Mother too in a sari at the school annual prize giving. There were balloons and all other types of decorations.

"What a pretty house Kala!"
"Shut up liar!"
"But it is so - didn't you mean it to be?"
"It's a sad crooked house drawn in wretchedness," Kala sobbed loudly.
"Oh!" the elves sighed, embarrassed. Kala ignored the sea of apology cards that flew in. They made no sense. They were part of a cruel fictitious world that taught her that dreams were indeed dreams. That was how women lost their virginity illicitly in South Asia. In a blind, brief moment when dreams looked real. The elves shifted uncomfortably. "Dreams are heartless brutes," Kala screamed piercingly. The elves pretended to tie shoe laces.

It was a good thing she couldn't see the sea of faces there. She might have freaked out a bit. The hall was filled with at least one hundred people. And Nirmaleen hated strangers since she couldn't see. So Amila and Kala told her that there was nobody there, only a few children from nearby schools. Really, nobody new at all.

The Flute Student began her performance. The performance where mother wore a beautiful silk sari from Karnataka. Where father wore a light brown short sleeved shirt with slits on the sides. Where Kala wore a pretty white dress that had a fashionable lace working. Where the Flute Teacher wore a soft shirt that would feel good for a hug, which incidentally did not look very Proper/Puny since it looked rather sexy. Where the Flute Student wore a yellow sari with an intricate work that could get tangled in the soft shirt.

And then it started. The flute sounds were like a new bride making small talk with her in-laws in between gleeful chuckles. Kala started clapping at the end of the performance till her palms itched. That was when Nirmaleen realized that her sister and Amila had been lying. That had to be a really large crowd. Good thing she had ears! Liars! But she smiled and hugged them. Years later when Amila watched a movie with his wife he would remember the hug from his beautiful flute student who could not see. He would remember how his shirt almost tangled with her sari. Did the blind hug differently? Of course they did. They hugged precious, Amila thought. They made some live in the hope that someday there would be another precious hug.

Dylan the Humanitarian as per findings of Kala

Kala experiencing hyper estrangement. Kala looking miserable. Kala looking edgy. Kala, would you talk about it? Dylan so sweet. Dylan estrangement sucks. Kala, uh, we can talk about whatever it is. Dylan I don't declare my agony in the open. Estrangement is an internal conflict. Dylan so caring. Dylan so loving. Dylan performing high on humanity. I'll see you later then. OK? Kala, are you listening? Kala? Elves made their remarks quietly. Kala in a bit of a bubble frenzy. Dylan looking on with complete confusion. Kala are you OK? Of course Dylan, stop making me look pathetic. Kala, I wish I could talk to you. Dylan, it hurts to breathe. It hurts to put clothes on and pretend that I'm a social bird. Kala, I wish I could have been with you. I wish I was yours always. Was that so complicated? Was it such a terror for you? Dylan, our minds are on different landscapes. They don't find a common requirement space. Kala don't bullshit! Kala, you are the queen of tragedy. Dylan, bubbles of obsession are around. They could hear us you know. Elves watched with hawky-sharp eyes that glowed a dim gold.

Kala I can't be your humanitarian anymore. Elves jerking their heads up in alarm. Kala I'm only just me. Kala stop driving yourself into misery.

Shhhhh ... Dylan, just go away please. You are not supposed to be here.

The Legal Proceedings into the Short Term Word Syndrome

It was the usual courtroom. The few benches at the back full of unknown jobless gossips. She was in the witness box. Conversationalist W approached her.

When did this whole thing start?

Not too long ago.

Nadia dangled her leg this way, that way.

The court expects you to be specific.

Conversationalist W sharpened his eyes on the dangling leg. Nadia ignored.

It started with the Short Term Word Syndrome.

Can you explain how you felt then?

I felt nothing. She shook her head vigorously.

Then you have no case!

My daddy will pay you!

I suggest you stop sounding plutocratic. This is a courtroom. What did you feel then?

I felt stupid. There were audible snickers. Nadia glared at the house and dangled her leg a little harder.

That was all?

No. She swallowed hard. I felt as if I was being treated like anyone else. And I'm NOT!

The court understands. What else?

I felt as if I've never been loved. And even when I wanted to. And the Castle of Perfection. Nadia sniffed.

Did you feel jealous?

No

At no point did you feel jealous?

NO!

There aren't enough grounds to prosecute Feelings then. Did you or did you not feel jealous?

A bit perhaps.

A bit or a lot?

A bit of a lot.

This is a criminal prosecution which will require proof beyond a reasonable doubt.

So? Nadia pouted.

Did you feel jealous?

Did you feel jealous?

Did you feel jealous?

Did you feel jealous?

Did you feel jealous?

Yes.

When did you feel jealous?

When Dylan compared me to just another girl.

Is she pretty Nadia?

She's plain as hell.

Did Dylan call her pretty, Nadia?

Yes.

And he called you ugly? He furrowed his brows and waited, as if this was the last ball in a cricket match.

No.

Oh so this IS jealousy. He looked at the jury. They all nodded their heads rhythmically.

Shameful. He didn't understand. Shameless man.

So what do you want this court to do?

I want the court to issue a restraining order on Feelings.

Very well. But how about your looks? Will you also need an injunction that will ensure that none turns prettier than you?

No. That will not be necessary. She glared wanting to shake him by his ugly white robe. Ugly man. There were audible whispers. Nadia thought she distinctly heard chuckles. But that couldn't be, because when she looked up they all seemed concerned and serious. Chuckles seemed like the last thing.

When Kala went to office the next day she did not know anything. She couldn't have. But somebody had seen, and when mother saw that she had been fired on misconduct (the nature of misconduct clearly unstated, but nonetheless so grossly implied all over the letter) she went pale. Kala walked inside the house – allowing mother to take in everything. As she slipped off her shoes she heard sobs. They got louder and Kala continued to sing to herself. If her mother was going to cry then *she* didn't have to cry no? There was no point in grieving for the loss of dignity at two ends. Kala sang.

Twinkle, twinkle little star
How I wonder what –

"You bloody bitch!"

- *You are*

Up above the world so high

"You bloody bitch! Where did you hide yourself?"

Like a diamond in the sky. Did she go flat on diamond? She did. She did. Of course she did. May be she could sing all over again. Yes. That was how it happened. You made a mistake, and you would repeat to get it right.

And then came the slap. There was no surprise. She was anyway going to get slapped across the face. It was just a question of when. She faced her mother. Expecting her to slap again. Likewise came the slap that turned the cheek red. Blood cells getting excited by the heat created through friction. Funny, she didn't feel anything at all. Just the slaps of course that left a funny itchy feeling. Very itchy feeling. The nagging type that made her wonder whether the body was still a part of her or whether she had successfully turned into an impartial critic watching the volleying process. The slaps advanced to full blown smacking. Until Kala felt rather dizzy. Mother stopped tired, and resorted to the less tiresome measure of expressing disgust over offspring misconduct. She wept burying her head in hands blaming herself at times and then blaming Kala at other times (mostly).

"There's really nothing to complain about."

"Really?" The mother beamed and hoped the other mothers overheard. "She's very good in her work and well disciplined." And the teacher patted the head of the seven year old clutching her hanky anxiously. A seven-year-old's dream is a clean record from the teacher. They spoke in hushed whispers among one another before the meeting and promised God various sacrifices in the form of cartoonless days and chocolateless days for a 'gudchyle' record. Some resorted to the hem of their little skirt to wipe off the nervous sweat. Kala's mother bought her popsicles from the school cafeteria to encourage good behaviour. For the next three years Kala earned popsicles on the all important parents-teacher encounter day. And then came Estrangement and nobody remembered the Popsicle Perk.

Rituals with Sumi-VI

"You left out the will?"
"You wrote the first sentence. How was I supposed to know? I just copied the words row by row."
We not sing again in class
We not sing again in class
We not sing again in class
We not sing again in class
"She won't notice. Will she?"
"She won't." Sumi giggled. Kala giggled. Sumi giggled. Kala shrugged. She supposed so.

"I wish you were my little daughter still." Kala did not reply. Mother the devotee of emotionalism. "I wish you were closer to me. Who is this man Kala? KALA!"
Kala listened. Mother loved to ramble as always. It was almost therapeutic. Therapeutic in scrubbing off guilt. Kala felt sorry enough to give her a hand. So she refrained from making retaliatory comments.

"I love you so much Kala - broken by sobs - you should have told me before getting into a mess like this."
Kala wanted to laugh. Who was mother kidding? "I'm sorry mother."
"It's too late Kala. Things have become ugly now."
"Things were always ugly mother. You just didn't notice!"
Slap!
Kala let it go. Mother the lover of children.
"Purity is the most important thing for a girl. Broken by loud sobs. "What the fuck did you do with whom?"

Kala couldn't say anything comforting. Mother couldn't know the pangs of obsession that scraped the mind mischievously. Mother couldn't know of a daughter that never seemed sexually capable. Mother thought these were the times they looked for a potential partner in marriage and dreamed of sex at honeymoon. Sex at Honeymoon. Mother, Kala lost her virginity rather tragically. Kala lost her virginity before marriage. Before Sex at Honeymoon. Owing to a severe and rather unusual condition of insanity/obsession. Such conditions warrant Sex before Sex at Honeymoon. Mother I hate hurting you, I hate being a bad daughter. Mother you realize I love you?
"Why Kala?" She sobbed louder than ever while Kala watched. Kala kept post on high emotional domain.

Father looked very angry. As if his daughter had misbehaved. Kala looked scared like the times she spilled food on her clothes. They followed awful ramifications.
He slapped.
She didn't move.
   He slapped. Slapped. Slapped. Slapped. Slapped. Slapped.

Slapped. Slapped.

"Will you stop?"

And they came harder and harder and harder until Kala ran away. Kala ran away and away. He followed wanting to slap more.

"Bitch!"

Bitch indeed. Only bitches slept during depressed times. Only bitches knew the art of luring innocent bosses. Only bitches knew how to get fired over sexual misconduct.

There were black holes all over that beckoned Kala. And Kala pretended to ignore them. Black holes. How pleasant they sounded in a not so pleasant way. Black holes here I come.

But Father interrupted the reverie. "Did you sleep with him?"

Black holes got blacker and blacker. Father's voice became thinner and thinner. Kala on black hole tour? Kala comfortable in her new found tourist capacity. Black holes are rather pretty - are they not?

"Bloody talk to me!"

What was it that kept knocking on her face so hard? Father's hand. The same hand that used to feed her when she was small promising her various goodies if she finished her lunch. She was very gullible then, she always finished her lunch in anticipation, but bonuses never came. How lovely child days were! Her tiny body could have easily slept on the black leather seat, and nobody would have even thought she slept.

"I didn't sleep with him."

Liar, liar! Black holes were especially designed for liars with exceptional sexual capabilities. Welcome Kala. We hope you enjoy your stay!

He walked off.

Dylan the Humanitarian as per findings of Kala

"Kala have you seen black holes ever?"

"No."

"They are weird."

"What are they like?"

"They are anti-depression holes. Close your eyes and imagine black holes, they make you feel good."

She chuckled.

"Black holes here I come!"

He chuckled back.

Many months since the tragic discovery and entry of Feelings, and efforts to curb therein

"Mother see! I scored the highest!"

"Mother!"

"Mother!"

"Mother!"

"Mother!"

Nadia had danced away in her tiny dress waiting to show the report card.

"Have to rush. Kiss for me?"

Kiss mother. That was when estrangement had walked in. That was when Nadia had been born. Till then it had only been Naa-dia. Naa-dia stood for the following:

a) Ability to talk without infusing sarcasm.

b) Ability to respond without bitterness.

c) Ability to be happy with her circumstances.

Humans had this uncanny habit of revealing the most important and ground-cracking fact last. For excitement and all other purposes. So. The ability to be happy with her circumstances was the most important and ground-cracking fact.

"How are you baby?"
"Mother?"
"Yes."
"I'm fine."

Dear good ones,

This whole Feelings business and the Castle of Perfection have been traumatic. My soul has turned into a child with no milk or mother. I watch, realizing that this must end. I can see the emptiness about it now. It's empty. Dirty. Hollow. Bruised. I feel cheated by everything around me. Like they wanted to make fun of me. Only because they like witnessing loss. Trauma. Humiliation. I understand that whatever action I will pursue, you will not leave me at peace. Therefore I will do something that will make the soul happy. I sincerely (she didn't care whether there was any exposure of Feelings anymore) regret ignoring him/her all this time. I imagine you must have been concerned by his/her state of malnutrition, which I imagine must be the case.

May I also thank you for taking commendable pains to respond to my earlier requests? I'm touched indeed. Irony of goodness I presume?
Nadia.
ps: I hope you won't have trouble figuring out who 'they' are.

How have you been Nadia?
Hurt.
Why Nadia?

Hurt Conversationalist V. There is no other way to talk about my soul.
She buried her face in her hands.
But surely there must be a reason.
I don't want to talk about them.
Tell me how it hurts Nadia.
Leave me alone.
I can't Nadia. You will die if I do.
This emptiness is almost uncontrollable. She whispered and looked at him.
The Castle of Perfection won't come back. You know that, don't you Nadia?
She nodded and looked away.

Mother woke Kala up and asked whether she was hungry.
Yes mother, very hungry for love. Famished. But she only nodded her head and wondered whether mother had forgiven her already. How she would love to hold mother's hand and walk to the market like in the childhood days to buy vegetables and coax her into buying a chocolate. In her size 1 pink slippers and pink checked dress and hair clipped back by pink bird-clips. Mother would shake her head in resignation and buy her favourite chocolate and she would wolf it while mother bought the home essentials. Very hungry for love. I love you too mother. Mother fed her toasted bread and butter in silence but there were tears running down and Kala realized how painful it was to make a mother cry. It tormented the heart. And Dylan seemed like a superfluous dream then. Mother loved her. Loved her innocence. Sad, thought Kala. There was nothing innocent about a twenty one year old who has slept with a man she hardly knew. Was there now? Mother was right. Kala wept too. Because mother wept. She didn't want mother to weep alone. Besides mother wept for her.

"I'm sorry I hit you." And she pressed her hands against a blue-black spot on Kala's arm and kissed it.

"I'm sorry too." Kala thought mother stiffened then. Without any response to the apology mother left. Mother. Comeback! Mother I need you! Mother COMEBACK!

Bubbles of hurt. Bubbles of hurt and depression. Bubbles of hurt and depression. And love. Bubbles of hurt, depression and love. Bubbles of depression and love. Bubbles of depression. Bubbles of depression. Bubbles of hurt. Bubbles yet to be discovered.

Bubbled space with bubbled dreams. Bubbles that laughed away tipsily. Kala inside a huge bubble looking very happy. Kala being treated like the queen of all matters. Bubbles of frenzy that sucked out sanity. Kala in a state of high-level happiness just like she always imagined. Bubbles of hurt bubbled away. This madness to be happier every minute. Bubbles of depression got bigger and bigger like they were more important than the rest. The summer of the mind when it bubbled away with no awareness of reality. Bubbles of cruel dreams. They were the nastiest. Called for high-level delirium like the type Kala suffered from. *He touched me while I watched him. I let him touch me.* Bubbles of sordidness.

The Short-Term Word syndrome and what was left behind

The soul was sulking still. Sulked and grunted. Sulked and made a fuss about the emptiness. And screamed that someone should clean the mess. What made the soul happy? She didn't want the soul to sulk longer. It hurt to sulk. It hurt not to feel happy. It hurt to know that the Castle of Perfection was a lie that they made it up just to torment her.

Dear good,

I will serve kids henceforth. There's no sarcasm in this. And I hope you perceive the sincerity and the genuine desire to feel happy (or however you may choose to term attempts at curbing a sulking soul).

She hesitated then. With love? Perhaps not. Much too early for such Feeling expressions.

Regards,
Nadia.

Kala's diary: December 8th

Each time the mind slips into a coma I wonder whether I will recover. It's a powerful coma beyond good virtues and morals. Those teachings are like myths shrugged off by the super unconventional. Undoing the mind, layer by layer dreams of the unreal come to the open - a little self-conscious, aware of the attention being attracted. But full of power - knowing that the on-lookers are peasants - and he the king. The coma is strong Dylan. I have no authority over such frenzied fantasy. I remember every feature about you. How you command them. How you command smiling eyes. Is this attraction? Is this what they write poems and cards about? About passions beyond the mind? Passions that teach the mind to undress the being? I am the student of a teacher who teaches me to hope. Gush. Laugh. This is not the soft careless type. This is staggered. Scared. Short of breath. I learn to think of you as a lover. Passionate, protective, and intensely and fiercely caring. Fiercely wanting to share you with me and me with you. As if this were the sole method of survival. I learn to think of life as a haltless ride with you. No partition between us. Dreamers, lovers, only happy in sharing and demanding. I wish you could touch me while I learn these lessons of power and passion – you could feel then what I feel. You could feel that you could kiss me and touch me. I learn to live for an obsession that teaches me subservience. You wouldn't understand these. You are unaware of this power-passion mechanism. You cannot feel these complications. I think of it as magic. These are what the teacher of passion has taught me to appreciate. I'm too scared to refuse. But I feel the sparkle in my eyes learning them. You could engulf me. I have no objections. I might ask you to kiss me again and again. I have learnt to claim you within this coma. You claim me. Unable to be aloof. You know no more than I do. We are both students then, you and I. Sharing the obsession. Lovers.

SNAP loved excitement in most ways. SNAP demanded attention in the most helpless circumstances and made a complete terror. The Normal and the Happy line curled up in fear. Obsession received a quiet blow. Mind Elves remained unacknowledged. Work dismissal an old tale from the twenties. The plain background screamed attention. Refined Established Ties were suddenly raw and passionate. They asked how it happened. They wanted to know what happened. She stood silently and tried to look like nobody was involved. But they never sympathized with the quietness of grief. They asked endlessly. Somebody mentioned a stroke was the result of unusual stress.

"What stress?"

"The daughters probably."

"Well behaved girls no?"

"Well, I wouldn't know." They speculated. They wanted to bring meaning to an untimely stroke for a woman of forty five. They were the doctors of all known medical opinions.

"Must have been that work incident."

"What incident?"

"This involvement with a married man at office."

"No!"

"Very bad mark for a young girl." With a shaking head and a look of hopelessness.

Mother - Kala ties that had been Refined and Estranged till now, stripped naked and knelt down. They demanded all the rawness absent till now. Refined Established Ties scraped with long nails roughly till it was a mess of agony. A ruin of blotchy hearts. Refined estranged ties.

Kala watched mother die with complete frozenness. It gaped at her like a hell hole and made her feel like a child trapped in an enormous flood. She watched mother battling for breath and heard herself scream in pain as if she were still connected to the umbilical cord. Mother died instantaneously. Kala watched for a lifetime. Refined Estranged Ties were suddenly the rawest ever known. They screamed like rebels and torched up all nooks of Estrangement.

"She had been under a lot of stress over that."

"Understandable."

"How can she live after all that?"

"Understandable."

Kala's diary: December 10th
   The eye couldn't see the sober beauties.

Giddy-gone. Begging for sensationalism.
For love so shoppable, filling gallons and gallons of cocktails.
Flirtatious and pasty laughter.
Sober beauties present forever so long rap meekly. Mother had always been beautiful.

Kala's diary: December 25th

I lit candles today. Birthday candles for Jesus. Two weeks since the funeral. Two weeks of an empty house. Empty house filled with numerous food parcels and coffee jars. Crackers go off. The house is still in mourning. We had tea today. A shift from coffee. Celebratory shift I believe. Christmas tea.

Rituals with Sumi-VII

"How much water did you drink?"

"The same as you did."

She shook her head with a look of complete distrust.

"Sumi, you lost."

"I never lose in Healthy Bladder."

"You just did."

"I think you cheated Kala."

"What, I had more water in an identical bottle?"

"How did you manage to pee before me?"

"And the new Healthy Bladder champion is…" Kala waited as the ritual required.

"Kala!" and Sumi gave the Healthy Bladder Hug.

"But you cheated Kala, I know you did." she said between giggles as they came out of the washrooms.

"I didn't."

"You did, but it's OK."
"OK I did!" And she laughed sheepishly.

After the successful investigation into Binoculars

"What are these planks doing here?"
"What planks?"
"I saw the planks."
"I don't know what you are talking about." Dylan the Tactless Liar.
"What do you need planks for?"
So Father-II had seen it. Father-II would burn it. Father-II would make saw dust out of it.
"To make a tree-house." Dylan trembling in fear.
"Where? Here?"
"Yes."
"Without my permission?"
Father-II might clobber with the planks. Father-II loved clobbering Dylan.
"Do you want me to help build the Tree House?"
Father-II said *that*? Help build the Tree House. Help build Ifthemovieweretobe. How sweet. No thank you though. Father-II wasn't father. Nor Batty Baxter. Father II was the twenty-five lasher without a fatherly heart. Dylan tried to think what it would mean. Dylan could climb up the tree without worrying about being noticed. They didn't like little boys climbing trees. After all, he supposed mother loved him. He started nodding slowly. Father-II nodded and laughed. Dylan joined in with caution.

The Short-Term Word syndrome and the Real Friend at Four

"The hanky please."

Nadia pretended not to hear. The hanky was a pretty one. Just the other day hankies were the topic of conversation with a special focus on Nadia's. Hers were prettier. Some put it enviously. Envy was present even at that age. If it concerned hankies.

"The hanky please!"

Nadia ignored. So the real friend went looking for other hanky donors. Water spilled over desks and chairs. Hanky was to be the cleanup strategy. No wonder hankies caused such high levels of envy. They were strategically useful at an age when water spilled without authorization.

"See," said the real friend to Nadia, "Found two!"

"Do you want mine?"

The real friend shook her head.

Nadia insisted.

The real friend shook her head.

Nadia implored.

The real friend shook her head.

Nadia began walking away to a dry zone. What the hell was wrong with her hanky?

The real friend asked then, "Can we make flowers out of yours? Mine's too wet now."

Nadia brightened. Nadia nodded.

Kala's diary: January 4th

I stood there watching the fireworks parading in the sky and wondered why I was stuck in such complete numbness. Fireworks are pretty are they not? Boss asked whether I could come

out for the night. I didn't want to go. What could you do on a sacred night with a man you felt nothing for?
Was it for Mother, he asked?
No. It wasn't, just that I was rather grateful for the numbness.
Come, don't depress yourself like this please, he said.
Let me be please. I rather detest cheer. I said.
Mother wouldn't want you to be sad, he said.
I didn't reply.
You know things were not your doing, he said.
I don't know that. In any case you wouldn't know, I shot back.
He didn't say anything.
And then he asked, do you blame yourself?
Do I diary? Do I blame myself for an obsession beyond my voice, hands, eyes and resolve? So I shook my head.
Your mother didn't die to guilt-trip you, he politicized.
My mother probably didn't have the capacity to stage a stroke and die, I noted.
Stop. This is not good for you. He urged.
She loved me, I started to cry.
He said, I wish I could hug you.
Hugs are good for those who want them, I pointed out.
Please stop crying, he begged.
Let me cry please, I like to cry, I said, feeling rather important about my emotional capacity.
I'm sorry. He sounded awkward then.
And then I hung up on him. I came inside and started talking to you. This body is not limited to physical depression. Look at me – who could know what lies underneath is a mad woman, who feels nothing but obsession. So strong that I can't grieve over mother but feel a vague sense of loss? I'm grateful when I

can cry over her. It shows that I love her and miss her and am capable of grief. I wish I could grieve fully. Grieve and cry. But large scale obsession demands concentration. How long will I last? Where has Kala gone? This is not Kala! This is some sick pathetic goddess dedicated to obsession.

Kala's Diary: January 10th
> *The road wet by the evening downpour*
> *The vague glint on the tar carpet*
> *Shit! Nobody seems to notice*
> *The miserable heart that*
> *Cries without attracting attention*
> *If the sky had eyes.*
> *(that could gaze down)the road would get noticed.*
> *Misery! Misery!*
> *In the heart*
> *How I wish you would thin away!*
> *Charms are an old-time solution*
> *Can't soothe*
> *Fresh cuts that show off*
> *Ugly red bloody blood*

Averagehood - was rather outdated by then. Kala had forgotten childish fantasies. They didn't work for those who only intended to survive. Survivors hung to the cliff even when it seemed hopeless. There was no issue of pride anymore. Nobody knew what that meant anymore. (Or pretended at least.) Survival was rather deceitful that way.

The ticking of the machine that carried a thousand bulbs with it. The dish paleness that carried a dead expression. The stench of medicine of a thousand types that helped a thousand sick in the hospital. Kala ready to die. It hung about the nose and tugged casually at the nostrils. The dish paleness of pills that worked whips inside. A closeted space that kept the body alive. A young man standing beside, staring at the overgrown eyebrows. Kala on the waiting list to die. What the hell happened Kala, to kill yourself? The dish pale silence that sent thousand images of pain and agonizing frustration that collected basins of bloody tears. Dead toes that walked mythically sobbing for lost activity. Women died every year Dylan of depression. She's just one of them.

Kala running with fisted palms to avoid the terror of breaking apart. This sensation of being wedged between sanity and madness. This million year life that made the miserable want to scream at the world order. This madness to be with a man who didn't match passions. This hell that hungrily ended what a mother traverses in a state of pain-ecstasy. Kala you still look gorgeous. Even your dry lips. I feel freaked out Kala. I feel messed up. I almost wish I was insane like you. I wish I cried with you Kala.

Kala lost between reality and cruel fiction. Kala the zombie of obsession who only cared to end this electric pain that bit ravenously on all levels of happiness. This madness that demanded an end - this sacrifice for eternal sanity. Kala, I'm messed up. What killed you Kala? Women couldn't possibly back out of their journey of depression Dylan. The end is a chaotic one Dylan. It was simple Dylan. Women died every year. No Kala! Fuck this dish paleness. Fuck you.

"Ole rite but you sit there OK?"

"Nooooo! I want the pink chair!"
"And what seems to be the problem here?"
Perfectly synchronized head movement to indicate no.
Nadia smiled. Little fools thought *No* was the magic answer. It was.
"Then please be seated."
"Yes ma'am." Perfectly synchronized lip movement.
"What's the letter after S?"
They all furrowed eyebrows the way chess lords did, deep in thought. Trying to command her senses to the mammoth task of remembering what every mother teaches her two year old to avoid pre-school humiliation.
Then came sounds
"Ter..."
"Ta..."
"T?"
"T!"

Some thought Kala killed herself because of mother's sudden and untimely death. Rumour spread about workplace behaviour. People who felt bad about mother's sudden demise felt bad about the suicide. Felt bad about rumours. However true they were. They forgave bad behaviour. What better way to prove admission of guilt than commit suicide? And a pretty girl at that. Some called bad behaviour generic with age in a casual way. A very few. Some hoped Kala would live. Some said Kala was on the brink of death with no true knowledge of Kala's condition. Some guessed Kala was in a faraway asylum receiving lifetime treatment.
Kala lived.

Kala didn't kill herself for mother and bad behaviour. Some

said they heard loud yelps in the aftermath of the mother's death which they knew to be Kala's voice. Kala killed for acute and unbearable pain that taught her that suicide was a way out. A way to teach the soul that tears didn't have to be anymore. Nirmaleen hoped Kala would live. Nirmaleen and a few others prayed that Kala might recover. Kala's speedy recovery became a common prayer on the lips. The extreme religious who thought Kala had been sinful asked God to forgive her.
God heard.

Kala lived. Kala didn't try to change opinion. Kala tried to kill herself because mother died. OK. So be it. Some said Kala will go abroad to live with relatives there quietly. Kala returned home one month after trying to kill herself with no arrangements to flee the country.

Kala suggested it. He offered a side ways glance – *an are you off?* glance. She ignored and explained the benefits. You could taste all the types that way, she said. He agreed then. And then took a long time to return. She wondered whether he liked the plan after all. But he came back.
"How many types did you buy?"
"All!"
"What?"
"What? You have a problem?"
"Nope."
"Start."
So they started. One by one the wrappers came off. "What flavour was that?"
"None of your business."

There was just one of that - you moron! I wanted to taste it!"
"Oh you poor thing! It's gone. See?" And Kala opened her mouth to show that the toffee was gone.

"Go to your room!"
He stared back. There was no indignation then because there was no energy. Or maybe just the shock of discovering that dignity could be slashed into tiny pieces.
"Go! Now!"
That night he went to his room and drew a man that in his mind looked a lot like Father-II.

And so began rituals that recuperated sanity. Paper shredding. Father-II's face shredded to tiny little pieces until they were too tiny to hold their ground. When he heard that Kala tried killing herself he searched for clues in their past conversations where she had shown such signs. It couldn't have been worse than over twenty-five belt lashes daily. And if Kala knew that Dylan looked at the issue belittlingly she could have easily lashed him twenty five times or more.

"It wasn't as you predicted!"
"And that somehow makes you more intelligent, is it?" shot back the committed boyfriend.
Kala laughed, because she knew she was beaten.
"Look! There's a butterfly!"
"Liar!"
"There's a little bird there!"
She punched him then.
"No but there is! Check before it goes off, hurry!"

She turned and caught a glimpse of a dark brown flying thing.
"Kiss me!" the committed boyfriend demanded.

She started giggling. Until it became uncontrollable. Until she looked all red. She looked up in half anxiety to check for signs of anger. None.
"OK, close your eyes!"
"You will?"
"You don't want to?"
"I want to."
She tiptoed and kissed softly - almost like a ballet dance kiss. The type meant to portray a graceful ballerina.
"Thank you!"
She returned to her giggles till he stopped. He kissed full.

Kala's diary: February 17th

How easy it is to love someone you are not in love with! Easy to pretend that you are a lover who has always loved. We played hangman today. He won more than I. I laughed more than he. He kissed more than I. How deceptive it is to close eyes while being kissed. You can imagine that you're somewhere else and not feel kissed at all. Imagine, this luster of the moment that covers up years of conflict in the mind. This thing they call happiness such a curse in the mind. But he makes me laugh. It rings my heart. It makes funny noises in my mind. He's my torch bearer out of this tunnel. I'm cautious with nothings. I talk substance now. I ask things that matter. I flirt with a vengeance. I call out names of endearment. I'm so easily in love. My spirit in deep sleep with no rude awakening. He's sweet and wonderful. He bought me my favourite music today.

They walked home that night. Memories lined up in frenzy on the offensive. Nobody to tell her that memories were trying to make her cry. When they held hands she remembered how Dylan walked her home after the movie. She didn't even want to talk to him in the bus. How droll that was! And now she was walking home with her committed boyfriend and Dylan was who back then? Nobody. Was he not? She called him Dy-len then and not Dy-lan. But when was he nobody Kala? When he walked her home. He was never nobody Kala. There was no timeframe for the man. Was there? He came and went. He was an incident. Dylan visits to Kala sends Citizens mad. Out-of-proportion-mad.

Two years later at a dinner with the committed boyfriend he asked, would she yes? She yesed. Besides how could she no? Funny all the mind remembered were mud pools and bushes. The friends the mind had for company. What did Dylan think of colours? He thought they were little wizards. What was Dylan's excuse for sounding rude in public? Because he was always too bored to care. She remembered. Sad. The spirit never grew up. Too petted at early breakdowns. Too much attention. Maybe sensible mothers were actually sensible. There was gratitude. What was gratitude compared to love? Gratitude searched for reasons to love. There would be something, oh search! Sweet comparisons, what no one else did, what no one else cared to do. Things known to be sweet and wonderful. Dylan wasn't sweet or wonderful. Dylan did not know the passions of love. He did not understand that this was a compulsion that the senses could not break into. It was a simple fact. Like God made the world. In the beginning there was nothing. And then came everything. Dylan, the biggest incident ever. The sad story of an emotional vacuum that glutted away. What lasted were bad dreams, one after another lined up, to feed hope to a gluttonous mind. But there was nothing sinful about gratitude. She yesed and kissed him. Soon she would be married to her committed, sweet and wonderful boyfriend.

The wedding was a little weird wasn't it? She asked. She didn't like such fussy ceremonies. She liked rain. She liked to picture getting married, just the two of them. Near a fountain, beneath rain drops. Fill the oath with rain kisses. Laugh till throats could only whisper. Wear flowers. Lots of them. Wild ones. And hold hands and run till hearts went breathless, and had room only to lie close. But the wedding was just as it was supposed to be. Kala felt old at the wedding in heavy hosiery. So it was. Like they planned in weddings in big halls with all relatives known. Weddings were after all Everything.

"Kala looks very pretty no?" Some nosy, well-meaning relative. What, after all that dally she played, this was totally unexpected. Lucky girl. Must be a very understanding man, no? Who would like to marry a girl with such a tainted past?

"Akka, you love him a lot?"

"Hmmm. Love is such a quaint feeling Nee."

"It hurts?"

"It kills." Softly.

"Akka!"

"Happiness."

"Aren't you happy Akka?"

"Love teaches the soul to attain maturity. What's happy about adulthood?"

"Akka, you can't be this bitter about what's gone."
"I'm not darling."
"Promise you will call me everyday?"
"I will."

"Remember the games I used to play with you?"
"How can I not? I fell in love with that girl!"
That girl is half-real. She used you.
"They kept me alive."
"Are you OK? Wedding cold feet?"
"No. You?" Kala asked, laughing. Nonchalant.
"No. Feeling rather warm in all this." He was in a striking black tuxedo that showed off a broad build and made him look more mature than usual. He winked.
"I don't wink sexy. So I choose to abstain. She probably pities you for marrying a psycho like me." Kala said looking at a relative, in a crimson sari and bulky gold jewelry, who kept shifting glances.
"Well, I take pleasure in making psychological errors."
"You look very good."
"So do you Kala."
"I hope it rains."
"Tell me about this obsession with rain."
"It's age old."
"Too long to talk about?"
"Too many people are in it."
"Oh OK."
"Some other time."

On a cool mid afternoon a young woman by the name of Nadia (at some early stages of her life affectionately referred to as Na-dee) discovers happiness. Happiness was a thin veil of nothingness that was borderline fictitious. Laughter and naivety were its faithful agents. On a mid cold afternoon a young woman laughs with children - the mammoth soul cleansing exercise that exhausted the body. But was this the meaning of life? Some plaster peeled state funded school in the suburbs to the rescue. Among the children so passionately loved by parents that she cared nothing for? But this was happiness. Among strangers that knew nothing of a young woman. A woman with no identity. A woman with no tormenting dreams. Just a young woman whose name didn't carry weight amongst peers, because peers were too young for that. The breeze creeps in, just a little. The young laughter was a minor purification machine at work.

"And what may I ask is this?" Nadia asked gently.

"You don't know?" And she widened her eyes. And then she looked sad, as if she felt sorry for Nadia.

"It's the ay-fee!"

"OK. What is the ay-fee?"

"It's a big place." And then she raised her hand. To indicate height Nadia thought.

"And it's called the ay-fee?"

"Ye-ah." Ye-ah in tones of that should be explanation.

"Where is this?" Nadia demanded finally losing all forms of mature diplomacy.

"Pa-risssz!"

Oh, so the tower. Eiffel.

Rituals with Sumi-VIII

"It's not my turn to wink."

"You *don't* wink anyway."

"What do you think I do then?"

"Bore him to death."

"You really think I have no sex appeal?" Kala waited for Judge Sumi to issue verdict.

Judge Sumi shirked judicial duties.

Kala took a deep breath. "OK. I'll wink. But what if he winks back?" Kala voiced fears.

Judge Sumi speaking words of wisdom: "It comes on the spur, doesn't it?"

"Yeah," Kala nodded. "Yeah of course."

Wink 1: FAILS. Recipient unaware.

Wink 2: FAILS. Recipient unaware.

Wink 3: FAILS. Wink recipient confronted by mobile phone.

Wink 4: FAILS. Wink recipient's position post - mobile confrontation is not favorable.

Kala changes position. Judge Sumi laughs away.

Wink 5: NOTICED. Recipient smiles. Winks back professionally. Kala freaks out. Smiles back shyly.

Judge Sumi's verdict: "Pathetic."

The Short-Term Word Syndrome and what was left behind after what was left behind

Some people were born with the natural capacity to love. Were they not? That was how they radiated warmth while the cursed bitches basked stealthily.

"See the way Naadee runs! Long legs!"

Naadee heard and showed off long legs as if casually. Naadee bounced away and waited.

"Naadee my girl no?" Mother looking into the face.

"No! Naadee *my* girl! No?" Father looking into the face.

Dear Good,

Do you think my soul is a stupi-dumb idiot who doesn't understand that this is all for the sake of you? I had longlegs you know - mother said I will be a sprinter! A you sprinter. A very you sprinter. I dropped the baton once and stayed away from sprinting. It slipped. I picked and ran, but they were frigging edgy about it. As if I did it deliberately.

I'm not born with the natural capacity to love and survive. How sad this bloody life is? No opening to experience purity. To look at clear eyes of children and laugh back with the same silveriness. The soul doesn't accept this incapacity to love you - you probably bitch about me! But I won't let you win. I won't. You'll see.
Nadia

Dylan the Humanitarian as per findings of Kala

"When did you last cry?"

"Why do want to know?"

"When did you last cry?"

"Are you studying emotional patterns of women?"

"Maybe."

"And you thought I will co-operate?"

"When did you last cry?" They were pasting the posters for the Church Cheap Fair. Kala started rubbing glue really hard. Kala Mind Elves stood in straight lines, their mouths set in thin lines.

Kala should not divulge emotional patterns, Elves opined between themselves.

"Last night."

"Why?"

"Because I wanted to."

"You should have called and spoken to someone about it."

"Who?"

He shrugged.

Kala's diary: July 3rd

The heart feels so dead, stuck in these miserable times. I feel dead. I need to talk to you. The pathetic whore needs to be re-energized. A pat. A caress. An indication. The poor whore. And now this very moment I can't think straight. The body, I believe functions. I have no news about physical discrepancies. The body operates out of compulsion. I'm seeing this man, who looks into all my emotional needs. And kisses me as if I were the most precious gift he ever got. But he doesn't understand my spirit. He doesn't understand that I take intense joy in looking at your eyes. Or matching glances with you. Or holding your eyes in mine. He can't see that no entrapment is tough enough to keep my spirit away from you. Do you know that when my spirit is bored - it counts the lashes on your eyes - the brown tinged black eyes - for kicks it says, but I know better! My spirit hates any thought unconnected to you - even if it's bored. So lash counting. I swear your eyes know more than you do. They respect my lunacy. They have come to know my spirit and exchanged visits. They know that I'm a sick pathetic lunatic who has only learnt to revel in you. Who sees you as an odd form of god that keeps me alive. What if you die? Like Sumi did. Or mother did. My spirit will tear the walls down. Will tear me down.

He kisses me. He loves me. He says he knows me. He says that! You know every inch. You've walked every mile. You've played games I forbid other. You know the weather. When it will sun. When it will rain. But you didn't/don't know WHY the spirit lives Dylan. I should go. I just got an SMS saying he loves me. Should reply. "I love you too honey. So much more."

"Look Idda on the ground!"
"Yes."
"Are they not very pretty?"
"Yes."
"You don't like them?"
"I do."
Kala and Dylan were at the Church grounds waiting for others to come out after mass.
"You don't."
"I think they are the purest expression of love," Kala said dreamily.
"Hmmm."
"You don't like 'em?" She pressed.
"I don't."
"I want to have an Idda garden one day!" Kala giggled.
He smiled.
"I'll let you be a VIP visitor to the garden!"
"Well?"
"I would!"
"Who else?"
"Sumi." She whispered.

He couldn't think of anything to say.

"I think they are a way the soul connects with the outside world," she muttered.

"OK."

"You don't like them at all." She bent down and started collecting them.

She looked up again. "What flower do you like?" Small voice. Don't-get-angry-please-if-I'm-pushing-it voice.

"Don't like them."

"Why not?" Wide eyes.

"Don't find them attractive unless to attract dumb women."

"Pig."

"My favourite flower's you." He sounded gentle. As if truthful.

"A real *botanical* flower."

"I know just you."

She started laughing.

"I like Idda."

She looked up happy.

And he tucked one behind his ear.

"Flowers don't look good on boys." Kala wrinkled her nose.

"And they look good on ugly women?"

"I don't think you'll be VIP to my garden. You'll probably have to pay," she retorted.

He made a sad face, as if he had suffered the greatest in the history of Wall Street losses.

Kala was satisfied. "And I will let other boys come VIP," she goaded.

Dylan contorted his face a little more.

"Even the ones I don't know." More goading.

A little more. (Contorted).

He sat down and started picking the grass beside him. She sat down next to him with Idda stuck here and there between her finger passes.

Kala's diary: July 7th

I have wondered what it would be like to be really close to you. As if you were my own. You dependent on me. The way I am. You begging for love. Like I am. You escaping me unsuccessfully. The way I have countless times. I wonder what it would be like to be treated the way I treat you. To have you know my each smile. Each turn of head. Movement of hand. The way my lips form words. As if you wouldn't feel safe if you didn't know those. The way I feel intensely curious to know the components that make you. He brought flowers - tiny white ones - today. Because he thought I was down. Told him my period bothered me.

The Short-Term Word Syndrome and Conversationalist X

Quiet. Hush quiet. Temple quiet. Except for the bird with the audacious squeal. Except for the tree that couldn't help the wind. Except for the footsteps that only tried to help the floor beneath. Quiet and quieter. No voices. No people. Bare feet against the cold earth felt good. Felt happy. Felt at peace as if finally meeting after all this time. But she needed to talk. She looked around. Nobody. She sat down and watched the expression on his face. How beautiful. No sadness. No mark of frustration.
Conversationalist X please, Nadia requested.
Conversationalist X appeared, clean shaven, in white, with tiny bits of hair that grew on a shaven head.
She said, "It's beautiful, isn't it?"
He asked "The quiet?"

"Yes."

"If you like it."

"You don't?"

"What I think wouldn't matter."

"To me it does." She started crying.

He let her be.

"Can I come and live here?"

"Do you think you'll be happy then?"

"You don't think I will be?"

"If you think so."

"I will be, won't I?"

"This is a sacred place where good is commended."

"They will condemn me?"

He didn't reply. She didn't say anything. She cried. Breath that echoed slightly across the Budhu Ge.

Could Conversationalist X please go away? He wasn't helping. He was only being prying and harsh. He wasn't even slightly compassionate. Go away Conversationalist X - you bad man. She placed the Lotuses at the feet and worshipped. No reaction. Quiet and quieter. Then she heard incantations, praising Lord Buddha. Low and cadenced. Low and patient. Only the good knew incantations.

Lessons on Bubbles. (Acknowledgements: Mind Elves)

Bubbles taught errant dreams to the mind that had never been known before. The way that people would only if they thought nobody watched. Bubbles were an addiction that developed over time.

Specimen 1:

Dylan would be inside a huge bubble. Dylan lean and thin. (No other specimens available). The mind adored bubbles. The mind teased bubbles lightly and accepted any attempts at humour by bubbles as well.

Specimen 2:

If the dreamer were missing the bubble subject terribly, there would be Dylan and Kala inside a bubble. Being inside a bubble was scary and uncomfortable. But rather nice as well. (No other specimens available) while the Elves were unwilling to divulge, bubbles hurt, did they not?

Blank.

Did they NOT?

Blank.

DID THEY NOT?

Bubbleshurt. Bubbleshurt. Bubbleshurt. Bubbleshurt.

Bubbles were a sordid way of recuperating strangled dreams. So they hurt. They made reality look so real.

I see.

Bubbleshurt.

Kala missed the boy.

Bubbleshurt.

8

KALA'S DIARY: JULY 5TH

This place is lovely. It makes me want to leave everything and commune with the air and never return. I crumple withered leaves with my feet just so to know they are real. My Bata slippers are in a corner, neglected. So, this is. This is to be married? Happiness has little to do with loveliness. Loveliness is solid. Happiness not. Loveliness is made. Happiness not. What are these conversations in my head? Un-lovely. Un-lovelier than all the conversations I've had in my married life.

"Did you cut?"
"Idiot."
"Omigod! You did!"
"Idiot."
"It's ugly!" Loud laughter. With huge breaths in between.
"IDIOT!"
Who asked you to cut? It looked fine.
I cut and I think it's very pretty. And you are an IDIOT if you think it doesn't look good."

"It's uger-lee!" Dylan hissed.

"It's uger-lee!" He sang tantalizingly.

Kala controlled the urge to smack him across the face. And satisfied that she was tormented, he laughed asking innocently whether she was upset because he thought it didn't look good.

"No. Of course not."

"What do you think if we were birds?"

"Birds?"

"Yes?"

"Like the flying type?" he asked a little confused.

"Do you know any other type?" Kala asked back sarcastically.

"No. Wondered whether you got them confused with the swimming type."

"I think they have a separate name."

"Birds that swim?"

"You know - if we were birds we could fly!"

"Gee you think! Wow man! That has to be the coolest thing you ever came up with!"

"Flying is cooler than you imagine!"

"Wings wouldn't be all that sexy."

"Nor are hands."

"Conceded."

"I missed the rain today - and I thought it would rain."

"There's still time and it might pour and pour and pour. And you won't hear the end of it." He was making a paper boat bored by her loud musings.

"Where will that go without rain, Stupid?"

"It will rain."

"Sure it will? You buy pizza for me if it doesn't?"

"You will for me."

He held her hand then. And she told herself that she didn't like it. But there wasn't time for a full debate in the mind because Dylan reached for the paper boat with both hands that fell off his lap.

Kala's diary: July 7th

Rain drops. Rain drops on the face. The nose tip. The lips. Eye lids. To show off little bulbs of them. I wish you were here with me right now holding my hand to stop the goose bumps. The window blinds down. No light to see through. Oh, me the rambler. What a rambler I've become. Don't you wish you were with me? It's just me, hugging shoulders – what stupid teenage action. Teenage thoughts. Pre-pubic almost. But see, I have statistics. 21, female. Sri Lankan. Only the pre-pubic mind. Don't mind the mind now. Rain - so beautiful. Like the times I've looked at you and smiled. And remembered that smile for a bit longer. It's too cold. I'm hurting the wet pages with the pencil point. I remember our un-lovely conversations and want to run. And run till I will remember no more of this.

"I think you're right." Dylan said scratching his head.
"What?"
"About friends being better than lovers."
"Hmmm."
"If we were lovers I would call you so many names."
"You mean you don't only because I'm not?"
"Yeah." He looked at her as if that were obvious and needed no explanation.
"But you can call me names. I don't really like my name."
"What's wrong with your name?"

"I don't like it," Kala said, as if relating the greatest tragedy of all time.

"It's pretty I think."

"What would you have called me if I were your girlfriend or something?"

"I have to think hard."

"OK."

Kala waited. Dylan furrowed eyebrows in deep thought.

"Baby."

"Yuck!"

"Babster!"

"WHAT? She looked aghast. "You're right. I think we should be friends forever Dylan."

"O two?"

"Pardon me?"

"Yeah - O Two!"

"Is that another name?"

"Like Oxygen. Fresh air."

She nodded. "Kala please."

Better go in before someone thinks me mad. Newly marrieds are expected to be proper too.

Help from Father-II tolerated in the bid to fulfill Ifthemovieweretobe

"What do you want to do really? Build a Tree House?"

Dylan thought that was pretty obvious. Father-II presented constraints.

"We will need a proper mason to do it."

Batty Baxter did it with his son in the movie. Dylan didn't say

anything. He waited. Father-II ambled off. Dylan watched. What did he want to do? He wanted to build a Tree House with Thaththi. He didn't want anyone else butting in. He specially didn't like Father-II's butting in. As if this was a general project. This was a father-son thing. This was Ifthemovieweretobe. Uncle Nevil from the next lane came over with Father-II a little later. Uncle Nevil was not a proper mason and he was grumpy. Uncle Nevil gurgled good morning which always made Dylan want to stick his tongue out and run away.
"Hello Dylan."
"Hello Nevil Uncle." Dylan smiled like a sweet boy.

Grandchildren would listen to the adventures of Tree House making with awe. They will be handed down from one generation to the other. Dylan the Tree House maker who loved a girl. The Tree House maker turned lover turned loser. Dylan did not like weddings anyway. They were peace shatterers. They had no consideration for the greater community who stood by offering happiness and best wishes for the weddings' sake. Dylan used to collect all types of planks for future use. For a huge Tree House that kids would have to line up early morning to gain admittance.

Why had no one warned him that broken hearts were venomous? Why had it seemed so easy to regard his feelings with such little importance? Dylan was a little boy? Oh, so, that was the reason. Someone should have told him that this was another game. He didn't know. He couldn't bloody well have known. Lost kites never came back. Nor did fragile loves.

"Will you call me sometime?" Nirmaleen asked.
"I will miss you I think. A lot."
"Will you call me sometime?" The heart was racing. Lumps leapt up wanting to break free.
"Won't you come and see me?"
"Yes."
"Come and see me, where I live would be nice for you too and there's enough room too."
"Hug me."
It was anyway time to go. The wedding was almost over. There were a few who waited to snatch the wedding flowers. Others were already in the car park. Kala waved at the remaining guests as was known to be the custom. Crackers took off on their course, Crackers announced the wedding fuss. Kala to be a part of the world order in a more responsible way. Estrangement was in the pipeline to be forgotten. Bubbles were to be denied. They asked about honeymoon destinations keenly. They asked about the cost of the wedding. They asked who dressed the bridal retinue. Weddings were after all Everything. Kala kept waving till they were out of eyeshot. They waved back. They talked about it for months.

The same night he asked, "Are you OK?"
"Yes, why?" Kala answered.
"Just, you seem preoccupied."
"No. Tired. So are you."
"Yes I am. But you look unhappy."
"I'm happy. I'm married today to a sweet wonderful man."
He smiled then and kissed her hand gently. Kala thought she heard him say thank you my love. But she wasn't sure. So she didn't say anything. She said she wanted to sleep for a bit. "It was

a long day, wasn't it?" she asked. "Why do people get married?"
"Because they can't live without each other. The way we are," he said. She smiled and nodded in agreement.

Dylan the Humanitarian as per findings of Kala

"Do you believe in that bullshit that eyes can speak what the lips cannot form words for?"
"You sound poetic," Kala sniggered like a three year old.
Dylan glared.
"I am sorry." She looked penitent.
"Do you?" He asked looking straight into her eyes.
"I don't know what you mean," she looked away wishing it was pitch dark.
"I wish I could fall in love Kala."
She looked up. Eyes incredulous. Eyes hungry to know what he meant, eyes wanting to delve into eye expressions, as ambiguous as they sounded. Eyes wide and alert. Eyes hard at work.
"Why?" Kala asked.
"It's a very funny feeling."
"What's the big deal?"
"You wouldn't understand Kala."
"I would Dylan." She touched the hand a little.
"Eyes carry expressions."
She nodded. She waited.

He looked uncomfortable then – as if requiring larger breathing space. "This is a little complicated – let's talk about cars."
"All right," she shrugged. He shrugged. She stuck her tongue out. He yanked her hair.
"I want an oldish car," Kala declared.

"Oldish?"

"Hmmm." She looked up dreamily.

"You're anyway a relic I think," he bawled in laughter. She seethed and wished she could cast a spell and turn him into a frog.

The Deep and Sad Consequences of the Short Term Word Syndrome

Nishanthi knew the day Nadia left home that she would not return. Nadia Baba stayed in the room too long. Nadia Baba talked to herself like mad people did. Why did Nadia Baba do that? Oh, Nadia Baba! The chithakaya was ready to burn the body. Bana started. Mobile phones were switched off. Relatives in white. Clergy in saffron. The chithakaya blackened little by little. They went off one by one. Twos. Threes. Some carefully unpasted hurriedly put up handbills of the dead young woman - those that liked somber ways of remembrance. Others ignored the handbills. Handbills were freaky.

Dylan unpasted a handbill and folded it neatly and slipped it inside the shirt pocket. But then the next day it got soaked in the washbasin. He never found out what happened to the handbill. Mother did laundry. He stood within meters of people he knew well. But nobody acknowledged one other; afraid that they might discover something they had done to Nadia. That would have been too awful to bear. So they just nodded or waved. Never getting too close to talk. He watched the chithakaya and Nishanthi shaking. Grieving women shook as they sobbed. Grieving men watched and partook silently in shaking sobs.

Dylan, if this is the last time we will meet, it'll be nice if you said

something nice about me.
I'd rather not lie to you my drama queen.
Saying something nice about me and lying really have no relationship to each other.
He raised his brows.
Really. She waited with careless hand on hips.
You've never wanted to find out Nadia.
OK. Let me try something nice about you. She took a deep breath – you are really nice to talk to.
That's a really nice thing to say.
Now it's your turn.
She waited.
He kissed her lightly and took off.

Only a few others were left by the time the chithakaya was completely burned. He slowly started retracing his steps out of the crematory grounds. How could Kala think white had no expression? White was sad. And sobbed loud and hard and made some want to run away and never return to the World of Funerals.

Kala read in the papers that Nadia had killed herself. A young pre-school teacher very popular with her students. The picture in the paper showed no little kids attending the funeral though. Parents probably thought that it was too disturbing for the kids, Kala thought. Poor Nadia. Nice kid, wasn't she? Of course she was. Kala told her husband that she knew Nadia briefly. Not very well though. She started reading the adjoining article titled "What Prompts that Stupid Move?" It was something a sane mind could never understand but would write pedantically in the papers about. And call it lightly stupid. Call it unreasonable. Prompted by depression. Prompted by loneliness and failure. There was something deeper than that. Something unbearable. Something beyond the grasp of what the world had shown. What could constitute happiness. Happiness became everything. Suicide had everything to do with happiness. Happiness was all a suicidal mind pleaded for. A thin feeling. A thin moist. A thin shaft. A thin hope. Suddenly the mind stares at clear space. Banefully bare. The Search for Happiness closes with a Thud. And they read between tea and biscuits whether it was unreasonable.

Nadia and Conversationalist Y

"Hello?"

"Yes."

"You look unhappy."

"I am."

"You must be happy." And then conversationalist Y giggled, "Or you'll die."

Nadia glared.

Conversationalist Y giggled.

"You are callous."

Conversationalist Y giggled. And giggled away.

"You don't love me?" Nadia asked.

"I do."

"Then make me happy."

"Not enough to make you happy."

Nadia smacked him on the face.

Conversationalist Y stopped giggling. Stopped looking happy. Stopped looking compassionate. Conversationalist Y disappeared.

"Come backkkkk. I'll take back the slap if you come back."

Conversationalist Y returned. Lips in smile. Hands in greeting. Hair in different directions. "Take back the slap."

"Thank you, you're very kind." She held her hand out. Conversationalist Y ignored.

Conversationalist Y giggled. And giggled a little louder. Nadia glared slightly. Not very obviously. Conversationalist Y giggled a little softer.

"Who do you love the most?"

Nadia deep in thought. Who did Nadia love the most?

She shook her head.

Conversationalist Y giggled. "No one?"

She echoed yea.

"You'll die." And before she could resist Conversationalist Y hugged her. Smiled. And hugged again.

Nadia wept.

"Conversationalist Y?"

Conversationalist Y gone.

"Is it difficult to love me?" It was unexpected.

He laughed.

"I didn't mean you," Kala wavered.

"Am I supposed to know that?"

"Sorry."

"Why do you need my love?" Dylan asked.

"It seems important. I don't even know why."

"Do you think about me?"

"A little. But not always." Kala looked away.

"Why do people work so hard when it has no link to their deeper needs Dylan?"

"Because deeper needs are trickier than they seem."

"And so they deceive themselves?"

"Why do you work?"
"I don't know. Social order I think."
"It gives your spirit a nap."
Kala laughed and started walking away from him. They were at the town recreation park where most young lovers hung out. Kala wanted to meet him because they were still friends, were they not? The recreation park was not only for lovers, Dylan had pointed out. Oh, OK. What time? Right after work, OK? OK.
"Dylan it bothers me, are you mad at me?"
"Very much."
"This park is horrible for conversation."
"This conversation is horrible."
"What if I have a spirit that doesn't enjoy experiments?"
"Your spirit is an unhappy one."
"Do you miss me?" she asked.
"Shouldn't have called you," he said with controlled calm.
"Do you think you'll be happy, being with me Dylan?"
"Some of us like the lighter aspects of life."
"Do you miss me? Dylan?"
"I don't think you are entitled to personal responses."
"This is futile. Are we friends still?"
"Does it matter to you"?
"Very much. Why did you want to meet me today?"
"I wanted to see you."
"It gives you a sense of relief?"
He looked up surprised.
"Same for me," she said and walked away.

❊

"Teacha!"
"Yes?"
"There are birds in the backyard!"
"Really?" She widened her eyes suitably.
"Ya! Blue ones. Prêt-tee blue ones!"
"Let's go and see them!" She clutched his hand and ran to the back yard. She watched how happy he was and felt tears well up. Damn! Why? Why did she feel so empty?
"Bye teacha! Father comes!"
"Bye! Kiss for me?"
Kiss.
Last kiss from Nadia going to a child, all lovers forgotten. Later he would talk about the tragedy of his pre-school teacher and tell everyone how he kissed her moments before she killed herself.

Nadia and Conversationalist Lover

"Is it OK if I plaited your hair?"
"Do you want to?" Nadia sat up brightened by the thought.
"Can I?"
"Will you be happy if I let you?"
"Yes."
"I wanted love."
"I'll love you." He winked. Conversationalist L started plaiting. Nadia bent her head backwards. "You have beautiful hair." Nadia laughed. Conversationalist L laughed.
"Will you kill yourself if you weren't happy?" he asked. Casually.
"Yes."
"But people who love you will cry."
"I don't care about them conversationalist L."

"Not anyone?"

"None."

"What a loser you are!" He winked. Nadia tried to yank his hair.

"Stop plaiting my hair Conversationalist L."

"You are a dictator without slaves." He winked tauntingly.

"Why did you want to plait my hair?"

"Because it's a pretty thing to do."

"You would plait anyone's hair?"

"Anyone who let me."

"Are you happy?"

"Do I look happy?"

"Yes." Nadia looked away as if it were a painful realization. She touched his face then and asked, "Do you think I could have been happy?"

"No."

Nadia started crying. He watched. He disappeared. Like they all did.

Amila married at the age of twenty-two a girl from his mother's hometown. Nirmaleen called his wife-to-be very sweet. Kala thought she looked ugly. Kala argued that she couldn't smile, even when she tried. Kala took satisfaction in the fact that comments like very sweet were dull and meaningless, ones that carried no meaning but a shaft of politeness. Nirmaleen let that one go. Kala said the Puny made wrong decisions because they were scared of the consequences of right ones. Nirmaleen let that one go as well. Amila was satisfied. At the wedding a flutist clad in a pink-gray sari played blissful tunes while sounds of restraint seeped in like a drain of waste water. She flapped lashes. He ignored. She flapped a lot during the performance. Flap. Flap. Flap. Ignore. As if flaps were common. Men stared at the lash-flapping flutist.

Amila ignored them as well. He shook hands with the guests at the ceremony in tune to the sounds of the flute. Amila's mother told friends that Nirmaleen wasn't only blind, she was also motherless. Her son had a very generous heart that pitied poor souls enormously. Rare, wasn't it, she said, a boy of his age that sensitive? Precocious among the friends suggested that perhaps the girl fancied Amila. The mother shrugged. It didn't matter anyway, did it? His bride had beautiful eyes that looked even more prominent that day through the work of the Kohl pencil.

Nirmaleen never bumped into him again. He saw her of course several times. But he avoided her prudently, since he was at a loss what to ask. Nirmaleen how are you? Would that have been OK? Or Nirmaleen what are you doing now? That would have sounded stupid, since he knew that she worked as a teacher at the special school for differently abled kids. So he missed her each time a bumping possibility arose. He forgot her in time. But the bumping possibilities remained untapped and he developed a quaint hatred towards lash flappers as his wife later observed. She protested sometimes, saying that it was barely noticeable about people, and he made a fuss about something that was barely visible.

Celebration of the Humanitarian and the Commendations therein

It was a solemn ceremony where all Kala Mind Elves looked as if they had received special attention from a nearby beautician. They hurried about trying to put things together before the ceremony began. Some of the more important Elves ushered him in. Others tested the sounds. Test one two three it went. Everyone was ready. A brief moment of anticipatory silence. And then some sensible throat clearing. Taps up the stairs to the stage. One of the taller Elves announced that Dylan was indeed humanitarian in his code of behaviour and could Dylan come up on stage please? Dylan walked up the stage - carpeted in blue, to receive the token. It was a tiny blue kite made of glass. Shattering applause. Kala in a corner blushing appropriately. Dylan the humanitarian bowed and showed off the Blue Kite. The glass shone as it reflected the lights in the hall. Kala clapped till her palms created a funny fire feeling.

Kala's diary: September 5th

The unsung heroes have never cared for limelight because it's not important. Being a hero was something special in a way the outside world could not comprehend. I felt it from the first instance. But rules like SNAP had taught me discipline. So I waited till a medical man told me that I'm pregnant. I'm happy. I'm rushed into a million emotions in a nanosecond. I'm frozen into childhood fantasies of motherhood. I'm frozen. I'm caught in a moment. I'm happy. My husband kisses my forehead. I kiss back. I'm lucid. I'm murky. I'm happy. I am to be an unsung hero of motherhood. I'm stunned. I'm confused. I'm nauseous. I'm happy.

"I got you flowers." Kala's husband gave them almost shyly.
"These are gorgeous!"
"I'm so happy." He looked bright and excited like a schoolboy.
"So am I."
"This is so nice."
"I feel so strange," Kala laughed a little.

He laughed back. "Really?"

"Yeah." She made a face of mock pain.

"Oh that is a big lie. You can't feel anything right now anyway."

"How would you know?"

"Why wouldn't I?"

"Because you are a daft man."

"This baby will be daft then," he said with mock disappointment.

"Do you still have those bad dreams?"

Kala shook her head.

"Tell me if you do."

"OK."

"You must always be happy during this time."

"Really? Then I can be pregnant all my life." Kala giggled like a child.

"You will be a fat mother," he said.

"You will have a fat wife," Kala quipped.

"Yes, and such a good looking man." He made a face of distress.

"You poor thing." She imitated his face of distress.

"You can ignore her and play with your child." Nirmaleen chipped in.

"You can all leave me in peace then." Kala revealed with mocked sadness.

"You can leave all of us in peace then." Nirmaleen laughed mischievously.

"Oh yes. You can make him a flutist and travel the world with him to all grand concertos."

"I will."

"He will start talking to the stars and be hopelessly romanticized."

"He will be saved from his mother's insanity."

"And he will always think how lucky he is to have an aunt like you

while having a mad mother." Kala paused for dramatic effect.
"And a boring father."

"Which otherwise means I'm responsible."

"Which otherwise means my child will yawn continuously."

He smiled resignedly. Kala lifted her hands in the sign of victory.

Kala's Diary: March 15th

I stare at baby pictures. They connect with a common sense of warmth. Common sense of everything. They cannot connect with my spirit. My spirit is still in a desert looking for lost ones. Looking for lost loves. Looking to revel in the tragedy of the heart. Looking for a man. Looking for my wild love. Looking for my wrath. Looking for what I dreamed of. I stare at pictures. And I see eyes like his. Soulful and soulless. Lost and strong. I'm a pregnant woman. What are these teenage lunacies now? Nothing. They have lost their real part. And the ghost of it pales my spirit. Tries to break into my Two hearted-Two bodied-Two minded space. I'm soulful and soulless. Lost and strong. A mother and a lover. I stare at baby pictures, trying to think of a name for him. Trying to focus my tenderest and strongest emotions on him. Trying to build. Trying to hold.

Tree House Movie: Blow on Integrity

"What is this Tree House?"

How many people were going to get into this?

This was going to be dedicated to his father. "It's for a school project."

They both stared baffled. "Tree House for a school project?"

"Yes." Dylan the hopeless, tactless liar.

Uncle Nevil started laughing like he was never going to stop. Father-II smiled. Father-II said nothing. Nothing at all. They both ignored him and went inside the house for a drink like Dylan heard Father-II say. May be it was OK now to contemplate how to get a ladder. He saw a ladder down the lane. Was it at the house that was still being built? May be he could ask the mason uncle there? He could. He could say it was for a school project. Mason uncle wouldn't think twice. Dylan went up the lane to the half-done house and asked for a ladder like a sweet boy with sweet intentions. He stubbed his toe against the ground beneath as he waited in suspense.

Kala's diary: May 1st

I'm not excited anymore. I'm exhausted. I sweat endlessly. I feel him continuously. It is him. Now there is not a speck of doubt. Now there is complete knowledge. I feel impatience turning shades on my skin. He kicks. He laughs. He plans his exit from his grand dome. My spirit sings music from my teenage. My early twenties. My turn of twenties. I ignore their warmth. For a nanomillisecond I'm a girl. Insanely in love. Willing to let go all other faculties to console and delight my spirit. Then I grow up. I call them a ghostly cold. I'm impatient for him. I'm energized. I'm stronger. I'm an unsung hero. I'm tenderer in my emotions than ever. I'm numb. I'm uncomfortably heavy. I'm a birth giver. I'm Two bodied. Two hearted. And more than that I'm Two minded.

"What if we get married Kala?"

"WHAT? ARE YOU CRAZY?"
He liked the complete atomic impact that had.
"We will have sex I think." He taunted in a casual-calm tone.
"Dylan, that is ridiculous."
"Oh, the world order is a little ridiculous. You'll get used to it."
She hugged her knees. Embarrassed, Dylan thought delighted.
"We could even have babies."
"This conversation is very yucky."
"Yucky? Babies are yucky?" He looked so dramatically confused.
"You – me – babies: are yucky."
"But if we get married we will have sex, that doesn't confuse you no?"
"Yes Dylan, IF." Kala showed her full upper jaw to say if.
"IF." He showed all his teeth and jaws. Then he twisted his jaw and winked. "So we will have babies."
"Can we discuss it if we get married?"
"We can discuss it if we have sex, no?"
"Dylan you are depraved!"
"Really? Is that a pretty word Kala?"
"It's called a Dylan word." She smiled maliciously.
"OK. Tell me a Kala word."
"Graceful."
"That's like what? A messy woman with no brains?"
"A little too complicating for your brains anyway. So try not to attempt."
"Kala, if we have babies, I'll feel so lucky."
"DYLAN!"

Kala and Mind Elves in Complete Harmony

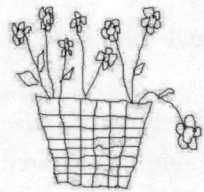

"What a pretty basket Kala."
Mind Elves sounded soft and benign, just like they should to a pregnant woman. One of the Elves said snidely that the pregnant were known as 'ladies' and not 'women.' Others shrugged. Rolled their eyes and scratched their ears.
"Why, thank you." Kala looked bubbly.
"I'm trying to transfer my drawing skills to him."
The Elves giggled really hard. Some rolled over. Others laughed till their noses went red. Some could hardly balance themselves.
"Well it COULD happen, you know, the transfer."
"But of course." This was a pregnant lady, they agreed in unison. They were not willing to run the risk of inciting her. It didn't seem fair. Not during this time at least, they thought in blithe humour. "The flowers are beautiful Kala."
"They are no?"
"Um-hmmm."
Kala drew more flowers. She spent hours perfecting them while the Elves observed them with artistic eyes and critiquing noses.

Kala's diary: June 3rd
> *He's redder than all the babies I have ever seen. I can't stand. I can't walk. I feel my body like a ripped mess. A crude mine with no glazing. I watch him. He has a name in my head. He*

is mine. He's my everything now. He's my lifeline now. They kiss him. My husband. Nirmaleen. Father. Father is proud of me. He has seen the unsung hero in me. I miss mother. I see her smile while I write. My mother. My unsung hero is not here to see this incredible feat. My precious unsung hero. I miss mother. He's mine. He's everything I live for. He flip flaps my heart. I'm a mess. Exhausted. Worn out. I'm tired. But Prasith is here, now. My heartthrob now.

Repercussions of Tactless Lies: Big Blow on Ifthemovieweretobe

He looked wicked. Wickeder than he had ever remembered. Many years later he would still remember that look and feel like a small boy. A very small boy. A very small helpless boy. Father-II bent over him slowly. "Why did you lie?"

"I didn't lie."

He grabbed his jaw and gathered it in his large hand.

Why did you go away? Why did you get a hartertak? I was coming home after school. I can't make Tree Houses without you. My jaw hurts badly. My legs hurt. The Tree House is for you. You're not here. He's slapping me like an animal.

Father-II tightened his hold on his jaw and smacked him on the butt. Dylan winced but didn't scream.

"Why did you lie?"

Mother watched. Mother watched like she was watching a movie. Mother felt sick, did she? Well, mother did nothing. Father-II spanked. Spanked till Dylan wished he had never known of Tree Houses. Till he remembered the Blup shampoo commercial. Till he remembered his three crucial decisions. Till he cried like a small boy. A small helpless one.

Careful, watch your step. To the son. Don't worry dad, I'm OK. Son to dad.

"OK, I lied. I'm sorry," Dylan sobbed kneeling on the floor like a small boy. A small helpless, fatherless one. Mother stood there, while Dylan sat there. She rested her palms and back on the wall and stood there till father went away. She washed him, something she had not done for sometime, and fed him dinner. Dylan couldn't thank mother then. He didn't want to. Dylan went to sleep thinking what ugly things these Tree Houses were.

Rituals with Sumi-IX

"This is slipping off."

"Well, get a pin and pin it."

"I tried."

"You are sucha baby."

"Will you help me?" Small voice filled with desperation.

"Get a large pin and come." Sumi indicated large with bloated pupils.

Kala tiptoed into her mother's room and discovered the Pin Box. The Pin Box had pins of different sizes. She picked the Tallest.

"Here."

"Ah this is good." Sumi nodded like the Grandmother of All Sari Pinning Matters.

"Now turn." Kala turned. "You must stand straight and push your boobs up." Kala stood straight and pushed her boobs up in the air.

"Now look at me." Kala looked straight back at Sumi.

"Now what?"

"Now we start acting like we planned. Do you have your script?"

Sumi the Director, instructed.

Kala picked up her paper. "I won't leave my children for anything!" Dramatic sigh.

Sumi playing Part Time Lover replied, "Well then our love is meaningless."

"It won't be if I drown myself."

"Don't my love, don't!"

"My life is a wisp of nothing without you." Kala stuttered in a state of near-terror.

"I can't say it properly!" Kala had objected earlier, saying that it twisted the tongue. Sumi had calmly shot back that, there was an element of poetry in Wisp of Nothing that should not be discarded.

"But I'm leaving my children anyway! It makes no sense then."

Sumi shook her head and said with a deeper voice, "I noticed it; it makes it all the more tragic."

"But I thought this was going to be a comedy."

"Of course it is!" Sumi cleared her throat and said as if it was a Top Secret, "Well this is a new type anyway."

"Sumi, will you be the girl and can I be the boy?"

"Why?" Demand-Why.

"I can't do the girl part properly."

"You are hopeless as a boy."

"Please Sumi?"

Sumi sighed strategically. Kala waited like a Poor Country waiting for a Grant.

Kala the Poor Country, Sumi the Rich World Bank.

World Bank in thought. Poor Country shifting uncomfortably.

"We'll have to swap clothes now." The World Bank declared.

"I'll pin the sari for you."

"OK if you're going to be the boy, remember to look at my boobs and sound really desperate," Sumi said matter of factly.

"That's what boys do?"

Sumi nodded and grinned. Kala nodded back realizing that she had learnt something important.

How Ifthemovieweretobe was not to be

Tree Houses became a mark of complete happiness of sorts for Dylan. He remembered planks, Kings of Sri Lanka, eyeing Ringo, casual chats with the Tree House owner from class. He remembered the Mango tree with the good seat, the nail box, Aunty Edith, the mason uncle. He tried to forget Nevil Uncle, Father-II and school projects. But for its overall impact, it remained the best memory since Father's death. Tree Houses conveyed a dream like warmth that felt like the warmth of a father. In spite of broken jaws. In spite of backs that hurt for weeks after. Dylan learned that lying wasn't a good thing. Lying involved cruel beatings and shattered Tree Houses.

Much later while eavesdropping on average conversations, he learned that movies were rather tricky even for grownups. Movies involved terribly complicated equipment. He also found out that there was something quaintly common after all. Movies were not real, just like Thaththa. Dylan never made Tree Houses again. Dreams were dreams. Some dreams were pure dreams in their capacity. The way balloons were just a cruel feel of a better play ball. The way balloons were stinted to light passing. Dreams were like that. Tree Houses with dead fathers were like that. Some little boys were born delusional. Some little boys never got over deaths that took place when letter F was being introduced. Little boys grew ashamed of movie making efforts and gave up dreaming altogether.

There were no trees. Just the bare appearance of it. It wasn't a forest really. Just the slightest feel of it. But there they were. It wasn't dark. Just a tad bit cloudy. Tad bit gloomy. Tad bit hard to make out faces. Tad bit tense. Tad bit nervous. Tad bit cold. But there they were. Tad bit uncertain, tad bit unreal. Tad bit -

"Will you marry me?" Dylan looked nervous. The Nervous Superman. She looked up. She smiled and took up his hand and asked,

"Can I kiss?"

He smiled back. It seemed like yes.

She kissed long. She laughed.

"Do you love me?" he asked.

"This moment is not real, is it?" she asked.

"I'm real," he prodded.

"I'm in love with you," she said in between breaths.

"Love is so pure that it only remembers happiness and lets go of bitterness," Dylan whispered. He touched her hair. "It's silky."

"Thank you."

"I'm so happy Kala."

"Laugh!"

He laughed and lifted her. "Marry me Kala."

"Marriage is a spiritual tie."

"Marriage doesn't die?"

"Marriage isn't real." He placed her back on the ground. Trees (or what looked like them) moved, as if on slow motion.

"Run home."

"Why?"

"Run home Kala."

"Walk me home?"

Acknowledgements

To friends who were nice enough to listen patiently while I read the first manuscript and gave me encouragement. The Loyals who proclaim that this is their favourite book. To the best Lit teacher in the world for believing the impossible-that this could be what it is now. To Cili, Ani and Ishi for the Beef Burger conversations: I hope you remember them. Dr. Dushy Mendis and Vera for asking discerning questions and for the hours they spent inspiring me. For shaping the way I wink, laugh and add sugar to tea/coffee, to my father - I still can't figure out why I support Germany at the Olympics! My sister and the oldest friend for standing quietly, but tall by me. To Ameena & Sam, for liking my work and making it so much more. It is so much more. The Greatest Hits of Yanni and Cranberries and January (my stereo set up) for the musical ambience and the perpetual pulse. *Thank You.*